Richard Carp

ROBIN OF SHERWOOD

THE POWER OF THREE

by Jennifer Ash

Originally published in 2019 by
Chinbeard Books & Spiteful Puppet
in partnership with the
Richard Carpenter Estate
The edition published in 2021
www.spitefulpuppet.com

Layout & adaptation for this edition by
Andrews UK Limited
www.andrewsuk.com

CONTENTS

PROLOGUE

Trying to block out the sound of Tuck's snoring, Marion stared into the shifting black and grey shadows that made up midnight in Sherwood.

Swaddled in a pile of warm sheepskins, she rolled over to face her friends. They were all fast asleep.

'Why can't you ever sleep quietly? Honestly, Tuck, you're...'

Marion stopped grumbling as a sharp gust of wind ruffled her hair. She looked up at the trees above her. Nothing stirred. Every spring leaf was as motionless as it had been seconds before.

Squinting into the dark, she felt the familiar prickle of approaching danger dance up the back of her neck. A moment later Marion sensed movement between the trees. As she reached out an arm to shake Robin awake, a familiar silhouette emerged from the trees.

'Herne! Thank goodness.' Getting to her feet, Marion whispered, 'Shall I wake Robin?'

The spirit of the forest responded with a silence that made Marion's head ache, his reply etching itself onto the inside of her mind.

Only you, Marion of Leaford.

Neither Robin Hood, nor his outlaws, stirred from their sleep as Marion picked up her bow, and followed Herne the Hunter, Lord of the Trees, into the night.

CHAPTER 1

A fire flickered in the middle of the neglected hermit's cottage, but it did nothing to warm the air or fight the damp of midnight. Nor did its occupants want it to.

This was not a hearth to huddle around while telling stories to lighten the soul on a spring night – although its purpose was bound to a soul.

One soul.

To begin with.

The two women, clad only in simple lightweight grey tunics, muttered over the spluttering orange glow. Their chant inspired sparks of livid red to join the pattern of light provided by the flames.

'...da nobis per spiritum virtutis Dei tenebris O dominum... da nobis per spiritum virtutis Dei tenebris O dominum... da nobis per spiritum virtutis Dei tenebris O dominum...'

Rhawn glared at the controlled blaze in frustration. Each letter of every word she uttered was undercut with a frustrated pleading.

'Give us power over the spirit god, Dark Master!'

She threw a handful of richly scented herbs onto the flames, watching them fizzle to dust through narrow, hungry eyes.

Feeling the glower of her sister's stare upon her, Rhawn jerked her chin up in defiance. 'For the last time! I'm telling you this isn't working. We need more minds to conjure the power to bring his soul down. *We need a new coven!*'

'We do not!' The reply was tight and worn. They'd had the same argument almost daily for more months than she cared to remember, yet the older sorceress remained firm. 'We are making progress. His soul and his mind are affected!'

'But not affected enough! He might be an old spirit, but he's strong. It would take a covens' worth of souls to end him.' Rhawn spoke more evenly as she eyed her companion. 'You can no longer deny that you are not what you were you...'

The crash of pottery as the nearest vessel was picked up and hurled across the tiny cottage sent Rhawn ducking for cover.

With patience as thin as a communion wafer, the sorceress rounded on her sister. 'The seeds of confusion *are* sown. He weakens. I *can* feel it. This very night he acts to try and stop his demise, but he knows it is coming. We need but one more soul to vanquish the forest's protector forever.' She paused. A smile that held no humour crossed her thin blood red lips while her habitual calculated calm returned, as if it had never been disturbed. 'You and I - and one other. That's all. Don't underestimate what the power of three can achieve, Rhawn.'

Throwing another handful of herbs into the flames, the younger witch, still unconvinced, tried a more placating tone. 'But sister, you are Morgwyn of Ravenscar! You were so close to bringing our Lord Lucifer to power!'

An enraged hiss shot from between Morgwyn's closed lips. 'We will *not* fail again. Don't you *see,* my sister? Last time our very numbers defeated us! Too many betrayers... but now, from within his own forest, we will destroy the spirit that halted the rise of the Dark Lord.'

Striding closer to the cauldron that hung, suspended from the ceiling, above the fire, Morgwyn swept her arms just above its rim. The flames, splitting into shades of red and yellow, leapt around the sides of the vessel. They darted towards her palms as she peered into the pitch-black substance that stewed and seethed within the large metal pot.

Rhawn hesitated. She was unsure if she should speak the words that had started to form on her lips. She'd muttered them to herself so many times, but never dared ask her sister the question she burned to have answered. Yet now, as the time for action drew nearer, Rhawn found herself muttering, 'You were left for dead, sister, and yet you live. How is that possible?'

Having braced herself for another outburst of rage at mentioning Morgwyn of Ravenscar's greatest moment of weakness, Rhawn was surprised to be greeted by a malevolent grin.

'How? Because my master protects his loyalist of servants.' The sorceress gave a rasping chuckle as the red and yellow flames blended to a fiercely vibrant orange.

'But he... they... those men, they left you for dead.'

'And there lays Herne's puppet's weakness, my sister. Only a fool would fail to check that his enemy's body had stopped breathing.'

Rhawn licked her lips, instinct telling her that, despite Morgwyn's apparent calm, she should continue to trend through this conversation with care. 'Robin of Loxley is dead. Herne the Hunter has a new son.'

As if stung by a bee, Morgwyn's fury reignited. 'I say he lives!'

The liquid within the cauldron glooped ferociously as Morgwyn railed. 'He's the same man within a different husk! As long as the ties that bind Herne to Sherwood remain, there will always be a Hooded Man.'

Despite every instinct within her telling her it would be wiser to hold her tongue, Rhawn shared her confusion. 'But sister, he *is* a different man. Robert of Huntingdon wears the hooded crown now. He has done so ever since the sheriff, that fool de Rainault, finally culled the one who humiliated you.'

The enraged curse that escaped the former Abbess of Ravenscar's mouth sent Rhawn reeling against the wall of the cottage, reminding her why she rarely spoke her mind in her older sister's presence.

Swallowing her damaged pride, Rhawn said no more as she watched Morgwyn's palms weave intricate patterns over the cauldron. The words her sister muttered while she worked caused the fire beneath to shoot upwards. Each flame becoming unnaturally straight and motionless as it heated the underside of the caldron.

The moment's peace did not last for long, for Morgwyn's anger still simmered towards her sister.

'A humiliation that may not have happened if you'd been at Ravenscar to help me as I requested!'

Stung by the unjust accusation, Rhawn drew back to the fire's side. 'And if I hadn't come from my coven when I did, ready to celebrate the victory you were *so* sure of, you'd have drowned where they left you. You may have escaped the outlaws killing blow by our master's grace, but I pulled you away from a different death. A little gratitude would not kill you!'

'Take care, Rhawn.' Morgwyn growled as she pushed her long greying hair over her shoulders. It had been years since she'd abandoned the habit of an abbess she'd used to disguise her role as the most powerful Devil worshipper in England, yet she still held an air of ecclesiastical zeal about her- albeit more suited to the crypt than the alter. 'You didn't have to stay with me, sister. That was your choice.'

'How could I go back to my people after that? It wasn't just your reputation Loxley destroyed! And now, after loyally sheltering you, stealing food, conjuring spells of deception to keep us hidden, you dare talk to me as if I'm nothing more than one of your failed acolytes!' Years of resentment suddenly burst from Rhawn's throat as she glared at her kin. 'I'm not such a fool as to expect thanks, but all I do get is riddles, with no real knowledge of what it is you scheme over. You demand my help but fail to trust me!'

Morgwyn clapped her palms and the flames relaxed back down into the bed of the fire. Her tone was suddenly as smooth as honey. 'Calm yourself, Sister! Huntingdon, Loxley – they are just places with men named for them. A man could come from anywhere and be appointed Herne's Son. When one falls another is chosen. If we are to be revenged on the son who destroyed my life's work, we must disable the master. It is time that spirit's strings were cut.'

Finally beginning to see what her sister planned, Rhawn leaned forward eagerly. 'You have a sharp blade in mind?'

'The sharpest. But first we need another soul to add our magic. Someone we can steer. We *must* be three.'

'But who sister, who do you have in mind?'

Picking up a stick of willow, Morgwyn stirred the thick mixture within the pot. 'The cauldron will show you, Rhawn. Look! Look into its very depths... *Puellae ostendere, Abertha!*'

As the two witches watched, the vision of a face began to form in the curdling liquid. The face was young and female. There was a shy but genuine smile on her face. Her pale complexion suggested she may have been blonde, but her hair was entirely hidden by the wimple she wore.

'Morgwyn, who's that?'

'A nun visiting Rufford Abbey, so conveniently on our doorstep. I can feel the strength of her pathetic belief from here.'

Rhawn laughed with easy cruelty. 'A convenient mind to mould then.'

'An innocent novice travelling alone. *Anything* could happen to her. Whatever was her abbess thinking?'

'And then we'll be three.' Rhawn rubbed her calloused palms together in anticipation.

Morgwyn of Ravenscar gave a brief grimace as she watched the liquid bubble and swallow up the vision, but she did not speak of her one fear. Instead she proclaimed with proud assurance, 'The power of three. That is what will defeat the strength of the triangle that keeps the legend of the Hooded Man alive. Three minds to battle three forces.'

'Triangle?' Rhawn concentrated on the cauldron, as she waited for her sister to explain. 'What triangle? The Hooded Man is held by his master and what else?'

With another brisk clap of her hands, the flames rose again, and Morgwyn bid her sister to focus her mind on the man who'd left her for dead. 'Observe the brew closely, Rhawn. What do you see?'

'Trees?'

'Yes… but not just any trees. Sherwood.'

Understanding filled Rhawn as she dismissed the problem of the hold the forest had on Herne and his son in one short sentence. 'A flame should do the trick.'

Morgwyn spoke louder as the fire below leapt up, almost engulfing the cauldron. 'Indeed it should, but not until the other element is under our control. The third point of the triangle *must* be dealt with first. Ah, there she is.'

Rhawn was transfixed as the vision of the trees opened up to show a solitary figure walking between them. 'But that's just a woman.'

'No sister. That's not just a woman. That's *the* woman. The one Herne's Son will desire whoever he might be.' Morgwyn spat into the caldron in distaste. 'That is Marion of Sherwood; holder of the most powerful magic of all.'

'Sister?'

'Love!'

CHAPTER 2

Despite the close proximity of a well-lit brazier, Marion shivered as she stood in the centre of Herne's cave. The vast space echoed with the constant drip of water. Rivulets ran down the sides of the ancient stone; merging together to form a stream that meandered from the back of the cave, out into the forest.

Herne was stood behind a large boulder that doubled as both altar and his place to work. His hands trembled as he lifted a vial and poured its contents into the bowl before him.

A sense of unease washed over Marion. She'd served the forest god for many years. She's seen him as both spirit and man, but this was the first time she'd seen him shaken, his movements clumsy. His presence seemed almost faded, as if only the essence of what made up Herne the Hunter was stood before her.

Is he really here?

Of course he was really there, Marion gave herself a shake. He was picking things up and throwing them into a wooden bowl. He wouldn't be able to hold things if he wasn't there. Would he?

'Herne? Are you sure it's me you want?'

The flames in the brazier swirled and changed colour as Herne mumbled, '*...ostendit vivum autem in tenebris...*'

Marion stepped closer as he sprinkled a fine powder into the simmering blue liquid that sloshed within the bowl.

'Only you, Marion of Sherwood, Marion of Leaford, Marion Loxley...'

'Loxley!?' Marion gasped. Her hand came to her chest. It had been nearly three years... She closed her eyes, no, it had been exactly thirty months and twelve days since... *Loxley.* 'Herne, what's happening? What are you telling me?'

If Herne heard her desperate enquiry, he paid no heed to it. His eyes were fixed on the bowl, and Marion had the strangest feeling that his whole consciousness was being drawn into the liquid.

'Only you can prevent the power that seeks to shatter the bolts against the evil one...'

Shatter the bolts? It can't be... Marion began to shake, but there was no time to dwell on the realisation of what those words might mean, for Herne was still speaking.

'...only you can prevent those who seek to tear the heart from the forest and pluck the little flower...'

'Little flower? Tuck who calls me Little Flower, I...'

Herne shot out a gnarled hand and squeezed Marion's wrist, drawing her to his side, so that she was staring at the peacock-blue mixture. His voice grew from a determined murmur to a shout as he groaned in pain, his words coming from faraway despite his presence.

'Heed me, wife of Loxley. Look into the flames.'

'But Herne, he's...'

Even now, after all this time, Marion found it hard to utter the words that confirmed her husband was dead.

A guttural cry of anguish from Herne snapped her attention back to him. In an instant Marion saw what bringing her this message was costing him. She forced herself to concentrate as the potion began to smoke.

'We are three, but weakness comes... Save the woman...' Herne tugged at Marion's wrist, his voice sounding increasingly as if it were being projected from another place rather than coming from the figure next to her. 'Look into the potion.'

Marion's edged closer to the bowl. The swirling mists gathering over its surface caressed her cheeks. The stench from the potion made her stomach clench and her head thud as Herne asked, 'What do you see?'

'I see... I see a nun, young, smiling. She's falling...' Marion found herself reaching out to break the girl's fall, but her hand was met with nothing but mist and fog. She saw someone strike the girl hit her and... 'Oh, her smile, it's different.' The vision changed in an instant. Marion's eyes began to water as she recognised the new scene: it was Sherwood. 'There's a bonfire. No, it's the trees! And falling antlers... and...' Sweat ran down Marion's face as she cried out, 'My friends... something's wrong. They're in the forest and... someone is with them. They're with...'

Marion slumped back, she couldn't say the words. Her eyes were seeing the vision, but what they were seeing was wrong. *It has to be wrong.*

Herne's grasp of her wrist softened, but he didn't let go. Rather than keeping her from running, he was now using Marion to keep himself upright as he whispered, 'Speak his name.'

Tears ran down her cheeks as, with a great effort of will, Marion muttered, 'Robin of Loxley.'

'Yes.' Herne sank to the floor of the cave, his energy spent.

Marion, half blinded with grief and confusion, crouched at his side, but Here held up his hands to dismiss her offer of help.

'Go now...'

Only hesitating for a second, Marion wiped her smoke stung eyes and fled from the cave into the comforting solace of the ancient forest.

CHAPTER 3

The mid-morning sun shone across the village of Ollerton, bringing a sense of joy to both its inhabitants and its visitors. As Oswald, the head villager, poured mead for his guests he felt, as he often did, lucky to live in such a place.

The birds sang in the trees of the forest to the left of the village, while the faint hum of monks going about their daily routine of worship, wafted through the air from Rufford Abbey, but a stone's throw to their right,

Robin of Huntingdon raised his beaker to their host. 'This is good mead. Thank you, Oswald.'

'You're welcome, Robin. To my mind, the Rufford monks brew the best mead in England.'

A muffled grunt from within the beaker of mead Little John was gulping back, suggested he agreed with the claim. 'They sure do. Any more in that jug, Oswald?'

'Oh no you don't, John.' Robin placed a hand over the top of his friend's beaker as Oswald went to refill it. 'It's strong stuff. Two cups of that and you'll miss anything you shoot at for a week!'

Oswald chuckled as Little John reluctantly lowered the cup. 'You spoil my amusement! I'll have one of those apples instead then.' As he crunched through the sweet fruit, John winked at their host. 'These Holy too?'

'In a way. They grow in the orchard by the old hermit's cottage.' Oswald waved a hand in the direction of a thin strip of ground beyond the village, dividing the abbey's land and the forest.

Much lounged against the side of the fruit laden table. 'I didn't know there was an 'ermit's place around 'ere.'

'It's been empty for years.' Oswald shrugged through his smile. 'Can't recall any passing travellers using it for shelter for many a winter now I think about it.' He picked up an apple and threw it to Much. 'The orchard belongs to the monks, but they've always been happy for us to help ourselves.'

'That's nice of them.' Much picked up a second apple. 'Shall I take one to Nasir to eat while he's on watch, Robin?'

'Good idea. Tell him we won't be long now. Do you want to go with Much, Marion?' When he didn't get a reply, Robin laid a hand on her arm. 'Marion?'

She jumped, as if surprised to see him there, before wiping a hand across her hot forehead. 'Sorry Robin. I was miles away.'

Oswald chuckled. 'Probably the mead, lass. It can take you like that if you're not used to it.'

Not wanting to offend Oswald by telling him she'd only pretended to drink hers, Marion smiled at their host as Robin explained, 'Much is going to take Nasir some fruit as he missed out on the mead.'

'Good idea. I'll go with him, shall I?'

'That's what I suggested just now.'

'Alright, Robin! No need to snap.' Marion marched off ahead of Much, leaving a group of confused outlaws behind her.

'I didn't snap, did I, Will?'

'Nah, Robin you didn't. She's probably tired.' Will bit into an apple, shaking his head as he watched Marion head towards the trees. 'She said she was kept awake by a headache all night.'

'Did she?' Robin frowned, 'Well, she didn't tell me.'

Hooking his bow over his shoulder, Much smiled. 'I'll make sure she's alright Robin, don't worry.'

As Much followed Marion into the trees, Robin mumbled, 'She's hardly said a word to me all morning.'

Exchanging a look with Will, John slapped Robin heartily on the back. 'She's a woman Robin, it happens. Come on.' He picked up the two sacks of food they'd paid Oswald for, swinging one over each shoulder. 'Let's get home so Tuck can get this lot cooking.'

The friar snorted. 'That's it, give me work to do the minute we get back to camp, why don't you?'

'You want me to cook supper?'

Friar Tuck raised his hands to heaven. 'Oh no! I've told you many times before John, once was quite enough!'

***

'You alright?'

'I'm tired, that's all, Much.' Marion pinched at her temples; the sickly aroma from Herne's potion was still making her head thud.

'That's alright then.' Much smiled, 'But maybe you should tell Robin that's what's wrong. He's worried about you.'

'Is he?' Guilt clutched at Marion. Even though she loved him, it hadn't been Robert of Huntingdon who'd occupied her mind during the remainder of her sleepless night.

'Aye, 'course he is.'

Marion groaned. 'I'll say sorry for worrying him later. Come on. Let's find Nasir and...'

A muffled sound ahead, sent both outlaws diving from the path into the cover of the trees. Their sense of survival from living in Sherwood for so long saw them moving to safety without either of them having to speak a warning.

Much whispered. 'Whoever it is, they're alone.'

Marion agreed, 'And Nasir hasn't sounded the alarm, so he can't think they're dangerous.'

Seconds later, Much relaxed as a solo traveller came into view. 'That's just a nun, that is.'

Steadying herself against a tree trunk, Marion felt her head spin and the colour drain from her face. 'Where has she come from?'

'The abbey, I suppose.' Much's smile transformed into a puzzled frown. 'But I thought monks were just men so how come...'

'Come on!' Marion hooked her skirt into her belt and began to run.

Unsure why they were chasing a nun, but following hard on his friend's heels anyway, Much slipped an arrow from his quiver, but he didn't latch it to his bow. He was sure Robin would have something to say if he shot a holy woman. 'Marion, why are we chasing her?'

Fighting the rising panic in her gut, Marion kept going. 'I must see her face. I must!'

'What? Why?'

'Just hurry up, Much!'

***

Robin dropped an extra bag of coins onto the table with a smile. 'You've been so generous with your food and drink Oswald. It only seems fair to give you a few extra marks.'

Weighing the money in his hand, Oswald returned the outlaw's smile. 'Thank you, Robin. We're very lucky here, with the Rufford monks so kind to us. Are you sure you won't have another drop of mead before you go.'

'I'd love one, but we'd better not.' Robin stretched out a hand to Oswald, just as Tuck spotted a figure walking away from the abbey.

'Who's that?' The friar waved an apple filled hand in the girl's direction. 'Unusual to see a nun leaving a monastery.'

John dug Will in the ribs to stop the comment he knew would be rising fast towards his friend's lips as Oswald answered Tuck's enquiry.

'That's young Abertha. She lived here, in Ollerton, before becoming a novice. She's been visiting her uncle in the abbey for the last time before taking her vows. If you'll excuse me, I'll bid her farewell.'

As Oswald walked away, Will's eyes never leaving the novice. 'Wasted as a nun.'

John gave his friend a shove. 'You can't say things like that, Will!'

'Why not, John? Look at her!'

'Fair point, lad.'

'Fair maiden.'

'And she clearly intends to stay that way, so behave yourself, Will.' Marion's tone was prickly as she and Much, with Nasir close behind them, arrived back in the centre of the village.

Recognising the hint of unspoken concern in Marion's eyes, Robin picked up his bow. 'What's going on? What are you doing back here, Nasir?'

The Saracen waved a hand at his companions, 'Marion and Much, they run, so I run after them.'

'Marion?' Robin reached out a hand, but she stepped backwards.

'I'll tell you later. I promise. But first, I must see that girl's face.'

Hurt by her rapid withdrawal from his touch, but trusting the expression of determination on Marion's face, Robin led the way. 'Come on then. I'm sure Oswald won't mind if we interrupt their conversation.'

They'd only taken a few steps, when Abertha turned around. The sun shone against her pale happy face, framed as it was, by a white wimple.

'That is a *very* beautiful woman.' Will sighed. 'I despair of women who give themselves to God before men of flesh and blood.'

Robin didn't bother admonishing him. No one did. All the other outlaws were watching Marion.

Clutching her arms around herself, as if suddenly freezing despite the blissful heat of the midday sun, Marion stopped in her tracks.

'What's wrong?' Relieved that this time she didn't back away, Robin wrapped an arm around her. 'Please tell me.'

Tears pricked at the corner of Marion's eyes, as she whispered, 'It's her.'

CHAPTER 4

With a thinning black cloak draped around her shoulders, Morgwyn left the confines of the hermit's cottage for the first time in months. She inhaled a long, slow breath of air, before coughing it out. It was too sweet for her liking.

Taking a broom from the side of the dwelling, the witch began to sweep the path. She couldn't hear Abertha yet, but Morgwyn knew she was coming. She practiced a welcoming smile. Her muscles ached with the effort.

'Good day Holy Sister. A warm one for travelling.' Morgwyn did not look up as the novice appeared on the forest path that led to the hermit's cottage.

'Oh!' Abertha started, clutching the crucifix she wore around her neck to her chest. 'Do excuse me, you took me by surprise. I didn't think anyone lived here.'

Resting heavily against her broom, as if she'd been labouring for hours, Morgwyn dismissed the apology. 'I've been sheltering in the hermit's cottage for some months now. It troubles me that I've made no payment to the monks for this comfort. As you're a woman of the church, I see this as a sign that I can now pay for the charity the church has unwittingly offered me.' Morgwyn produced a cup of clear liquid from within the folds of the cloak.

'Please, accept this refreshment to ease my conscience.'

Abertha backed away, unsure why she felt such an overwhelming desire to be as far from the cottage as possible. 'God has surely seen your generosity, good woman. Enjoy it yourself with my blessing.' She gave a courteous dip of her head. 'If you'll excuse me, my abbess awaits.'

The leaves of the trees fluttered, agitated as Morgwyn clicked her fingers, and the girl found herself stumbling forward.

'But you are *so* thirsty, my child. So *very* thirsty.'

Morgwyn held up the drink as, with a helpless cry, Abertha dropped to her knees.

The novice's hands scrabbled at her neck as her throat dried to dust. Desperate for water, she mumbled through cracking, parched lips, 'The drink... Please... I...'

Morgwyn's eyes shone as Abertha tore the leather beaker from her fingers. The girl drank greedily, her need for her thirst to be sated blinding her to the bitter taste.

'Ah...' Abertha sighed as the liquid nectar soothed her throat. 'Thank you, good woman. I can't imagine why I was so thirsty. It was like I was...'

Morgwyn's eyes narrowed as the novice slumped, unmoving, to the ground, her habit rucked incongruously to one side.

'Like you were dying of thirst?' Morgwyn yanked the wimple off the girl's head and threw it to the ground in disgust before kicking open the cottage door.

'And now, we are three.'

***

The spring sunshine felt tarnished as the outlaws arrived back at the camp. Few words had been spoken as they'd walked away from Ollerton. Even the birds had stopped singing.

Much directed an anxious glance towards Marion, who was walking alone to one side of the group. Robin, meanwhile, was stamping on ahead, his mood morose.

It was a relief to reach their camp. However, Tuck was not impressed when John and Will dumped their sacks of food and immediately went to sit by the fire.

'That's it, leave me to sort this lot out and get yourselves comfy, why don't you?'

'Good idea, thanks Tuck.' Will threw a log on the fire, more out of habit than necessity.

Tuck rolled his eyes. 'Much, can you pour this lazy lot some ale while I work on supper? The *weak* stuff! Oswald's mead was strong enough to fell a stag.'

Happy to help, Much picked up the ale pouch. 'You want some too?'

'A large one.'

'You don't say.' Little John muttered, earning himself a cuff around the ear from Tuck as he passed by to fetch some herbs for the pot.

Nasir flicked his eyes away from his friends towards Robin and Marion.

They were sat by themselves at the far side of the clearing. He couldn't hear what they said, but their defensive body language spoke volumes.

'Something bad is coming.'

'What's coming, Nasir?' Much poured some ale into Tuck's and Will's cups.

'I don't know.' The Saracen observed Marion from across the camp. 'But she does.'

'I'm sorry I've been so quiet.'

Marion sat with her knees tucked beneath her chin, her back resting against a fallen trunk. Every now and then she lifted her eyes to watch Robin.

His expression was a cloud of concern; his blonde hair had flopped over one eye. She lifted a hand to wipe it away, wanting to tell him everything was going to be just alright, but she lowered it hastily as the words stuck in her throat. She couldn't lie to him like that, not if...

Marion swallowed. She knew she was going to have to tell Robin what Herne had shown her. How he might react to what she'd seen, dismayed her more than he'd ever understand.

'Much said you didn't sleep well. You should have told me. You could have rested here today rather than come to Ollerton.'

'I know.'

Moving away from the tree against which he'd been crouched, Robin sat beside her, and stretched out an arm. 'Come here.'

Marion had dodged out of his reach before she'd realised what she was done, and then immediately wished she hadn't. Robin looked crushed. Her second rejection of him that day was doing more damage to his confidence than the Sheriff of Nottingham or Guy of Gisburne could ever do.

'I'm sorry, I...'

'Just tell me what's wrong.'

Robin looked so sad. Marion longed to wrap him in her arms, but instinct held her back. Instead she hugged her own knees tighter against her chest.

'The thing is Robin, I'd love a hug. I truly would, but there's something I have to tell you... and I know you won't like it.' Her words seemed to swell in her throat, refusing to come out. How could she tell him what she had seen, and what it would mean to them as a couple - as a group- if what Herne had shown her was real?

But it couldn't be real—could it?

His patience snapping, Robin picked up a stone and threw it into the forest. 'What is it, Marion? What won't I like? You've been fine with the others, but every time you look at me it's as if... Oh I don't know. I just don't know what to do or say or...'

'Please Robin! I will explain... but I'm frightened.'

'Frightened of what?' Robin's anger dissolved in an instant.

'Of ruining this.' Marion gestured to the campfire and their friends who were sat together, talking quietly. 'Look at them, Robin. Look at *us*. We've been through such tough times and I love you all so much. You most of all.'

Reaching forward, Robin took her hand; relieved when she didn't pull it away. 'And I love you too.'

'But now we have to face it again! How long before someone sitting around that campfire right now doesn't survive what we might encounter tomorrow, or the next day, or the one after that? Think of those,' she paused, considering the next words carefully, "we've had to send away."

Robin shook his head. That was not a thought either of them could afford to have.

Instead, he asked, 'Face what again? What did you see today Marion? What was it about that novice that worried you?'

'I'm not sure. I don't know how to start.'

'I think you'd better have that hug after all.' As Robin drew her in next to him, he could feel her trembling. 'You really are afraid, aren't you? I can't remember the last time you were this shaken.'

Marion let out a long exhalation of breath. 'If I tell you, will you promise not to let go of my hand?'

'Why would I ever want to let go of you?'

'Please... just promise me, Robin.'

'I promise.'

CHAPTER 5

'Will the nun sleep for long?' Rhawn poked her foot at the crouched figure of Abertha sprawled on the cottage's floor.

'Until I decide otherwise.' Morgwyn selected a clay bowl from a collection on a table near the fire and lodged it over the rim of the cauldron. Spreading her hands over the pot, she threw her head back, her eyes wide and eager as she beseeched her master.

'Lord Lucifer, curse this vessel so we may destroy the soul of the forest, and so work to release you from the binding earth of the Underworld!' She turned to her sister, beckoning with ill-tempered urgency. 'Pass my quill and ink. Quickly.'

Morgwyn repeated her plea to Satan as Rhawn scrambled through the bottles and pots on the table, unable to spot her quarry.

'For Hell's sake, it's there, on the table! Hurry!' Morgwyn closed her eyes, her forehead creased in concentration as she muttered, '*Suscipe verba haec tua est vinculum tenebris Dominus.*'

From nowhere, and out of nothing, flames sparked within the pot just as Rhawn located the ink and quill. 'I have them.'

Keeping her eyes shut, Morgwyn exhaled her words with a relish that made Rhawn's eyes gleam in anticipation. 'Drizzle the ink into the bowl. All of it.'

Removing the stopper from the bottle, Rhawn poured it into the sparking clay. Thicker than normal quill ink, its jet blackness oozed from its container.

As if seeing through her closed eyes, Morgwyn smiled her approval. 'Now, concentrate. Picture the woman. Call her by her three names: Marion of Sherwood, Marion of Leaford and Marion Loxley.'

Speaking in harmony, their voices melding into one, the two witches focussed with salacious greed on the bowl of ink, its surface popping with boiling bubbles in time to their chant.

Marion of Sherwood, Marion of Leaford, Marion Loxley... Marion of Sherwood, Marion of Leaford, Marion Loxley... Marion of Sherwood, Marion of Leaford, Marion Loxley...

With each sounding of Marion's names, the ink rippled fiercely, its viscosity thinning until it had doubled in amount, and was as silky smooth as normal ink. The noise of its boiling was abnormally loud, as if the substance itself was angered at being disturbed.

Over the gulping glugs of the distilling mixture, Morgwyn commanded, 'Pass me the quill, Rhawn. Keep chanting.'

Her voice alone now, Rhawn kept up the litany of names. Over and over she spoke them, until they no longer sounded real to her ears. 'Marion of Sherwood, Marion of Leaford, Marion Loxley...'

Opening her eyes, Morgwyn held the quill, as if formally introducing it to the pot. 'Quill so sharp, take this ink and carve the words of the Dark Lord onto the hearts of those it touches. Let us seep the words of your control *and* your truth into their souls.'

Rhawn was becoming breathless as she continued, 'Marion of Sherwood, Marion of Leaford, Marion Loxley...' The words mere murmurs now as she listened to her sister.

'Oh Lord and master, I call you by three names: Satan, Beelzebub, Lucifer... I beseech thee, aid our sight! Let us see what the woman sees. We call her by her three names! Let us use the eyes of Marion of Sherwood, of Leaford, wife of Loxley.'

A hush fell across the room as the animated fizzing of the liquid calmed and it lay, unmoving, as if it were nothing more than church ink, ready and waiting to embellish a scripture.

Morgwyn placed a hand on her sister's arm. 'Look into the ink. Look hard.'

Rhawn drew an eager breath. 'It's clearing... I see... Oh, it's just trees.'

'Of course it's trees!' Snapping, frustrated by her sister's inability to catch on to anything very fast, Morgwyn said, 'The woman is in Sherwood! We are seeing what she can see. Have patience!'

A second later the sorceress purred with satisfaction. 'Ah, there he is. So that's the new Hooded Man.'

'Handsome... delicious even.'

Ignoring her sister, Morgwyn watched as Marion's viewpoint changed. 'She's turning... Ah, there they are. Herne's hounds!' Her eyes flashed with hatred as she saw Robin Hood's men. 'I've waited a long time to revenge myself on them.'

'Why didn't we just kill them when they were in Ollerton?'

'Because once we have destroyed Robin Hood's world, the others will destroy themselves. The guilt that they couldn't stop what we're about to do will turn them against each other. Why should we waste magic on such scum?'

Rhawn couldn't see why that magic would have been considered wasted. 'But they saw the nun?'

Morgwyn smiled. 'As I intended they should.' She stabbed a fingernail towards the motionless figure on the floor. 'Fetch her!'

Kicking the novice hard in the ribs, Rhawn grinned as Abertha squirmed, drawing back from the women in grey; but no sound came out of her open lips and her eyes flashed in terror.

'You hope the outlaws will come in search of this sorry excuse for a woman?'

'Herne told Marion to look for her.'

Rhawn frowned. 'How do you know that?'

'We can both see through her eyes, but as the holder of the quill, I can also read his thoughts. They're hazy, but they are within my reach.'

'You can actually see what Herne told Marion in his prophecy, Morgwyn? The prophecy you adjusted before we hunted for a third witch?'

'Yes, although I didn't change much of what Marion would have seen. I simply added some of the more – let's call them, personal touches. Words that will wield a destructive power over Herne's thoughts and an image that will, gradually, chip away at his presence.' Crouching down, Morgwyn jabbed a finger at Abertha's throat, grinning as the girl tried, and failed, to stand and speak. 'Once we three are united, we'll drive Herne away for good. Now, hold out her arm.'

Grabbing the novice's wrist, Rhawn shoved the sleeve of the habit up past the elbow, exposing white, trembling flesh.

Terrified, trapped by the magic which held her, Abertha watched Morgwyn tap the quill three times against the side of the pot before dipping it inside. She tried to draw away, but Rhawn twisted her arm back, making her gasp with pain. As Morgwyn approached, the novice's eyes closed, muttering a prayer that her lips refused to open for.

'*Suscipe verba haec tua est vinculum tenebris Dominus*. Lord of Darkness, use this ink to entrap and ensnare, to bend the will of those bought beneath its quill. Take Abertha, daughter of the church, your greatest enemy, into your realm.'

Abertha tried to get away, but her muscles were like water, and all she achieved was to make the witches laugh as the spiked tip of the quill met with her newly exposed limb.

Writing on the novice's quaking flesh, Morgwyn proclaimed, 'Satan, let the power of your words mix with her life's blood.'

With each letter that was inscribed on her arm, Abertha's voice slowly returned. She cried in anguish as the dagger-like quill continued its inscription, but no one took any notice.

Holding the young nun still, Rhawn gasped as she observed her sister at work.

'The words... they're disappearing.'

'They are becoming part of her.' Morgwyn drew the final letter in place. 'You can let go of her now.'

The second Rhawn released her, Abertha let out a tortured cry, before curling herself up in a tight ball on the floor. Then, seconds later, her arms and legs shot out to either side and she went rigid; staring in shock at the rafters of the hermit's cottage before, limb by limb, her body relaxed.

As the novice's frame loosened, Morgwyn raised her hands and clapped them once over the stricken figure. 'She who signs a pact with the Devil can only be freed by death.' Then, with a snap of her fingers, Morgwyn stepped backwards as Abertha, bound in a trance of invisible enchantment, rose to her feet.

Abertha did not tremble now, but rather oozed with confident contentment as she approached Morgwyn. 'What would you have me do, my Lady?'

'Whatever I command.'

'Yes, my Lady.'

Rhawn grinned as Abertha walked to the cauldron and stood impassively, awaiting her orders. 'You impress me, sister.'

The former abbess inclined her head in acceptance of the compliment. 'Come, let's see what the outlaws are doing.'

Sprinkling some dust into the clay pot, Morgwyn's cruel smile made her haggard face shine. 'Ah, look. We're just in time to watch Marion break her lover's heart.'

CHAPTER 6

Robin sat next to Marion, his hand still in hers, as the outlaws joined them around the fire in the dwindling light of the late afternoon sunshine.

Tuck passed a few pouches of ale around the circle, as they waited for Robin to speak. They all recognised the expression on his face. It was one they'd seen countless times before. It spoke of coming danger.

Robin gave Marion's palm a reassuring squeeze. 'You have something to tell us?'

Not wanting to meet anyone's gaze, Marion watched the logs crackling beneath the fire. 'Last night I couldn't sleep. There was a noise and... Herne came.'

'Herne?' Robin wasn't sure what he'd expected to hear, but he hadn't expected that the Lords of the Trees would come to Marion and not him. 'Why didn't you wake me? Why didn't you say before?'

Marion briefly met his eyes, tilting her chin up in momentary denial of the hurt she was about to cause, but was unable to prevent. 'He said not to wake you.'

'Strange, but he will have had a reason.' Robin put a comforting arm around her shoulder.

'He stood in that clearing over there; beckoning to me.' She pointed towards the trees to the left. 'I followed Herne to his cave. He seemed... I don't know, wrong somehow.'

'Wrong, lass?' Little John offered her some ale, but Marion shook her head.

'Weak, like he was recovering from a fight.' Her forehead crinkled as she tried to recall the sensation of being out of place she'd got from the spirit. 'It was as if he was there but fading away.'

Will pulled his dagger from his belt, glaring into the section of forest where Marion had seen Herne. 'What did he say?'

'That we must save the woman. He showed me a vision, a prophecy I suppose. I saw a face. It was the novice we saw in Ollerton. That's why I was so desperate to see her properly. I wanted to be sure it was the woman Herne had shown me.'

Much peered nervously over his shoulder, 'But we saw her Marion, so she isn't in danger—is she?'

'She might be by now, Much. I don't know.' With a heavy sigh, Marion added, 'There's more. Worse. I haven't known how to tell you. Herne said something I've heard before. That we've all heard before... apart from you, Robin.'

As one, without even thinking about what they were doing, instinct made the outlaws reached for their nearest weapons, as Robin coaxed, 'Keep going. It's fine, Marion. You can tell us.'

Taking a deep breath, she looked at the outlaws. John and Will, each with knife or quarterstaff in one hand and ale in the other, stared back at her. Nasir, quiet as ever, his eyes fixed upon the flames was listening, not just to her she knew, but to the forest for signs of trouble. Much... well, he was a man now, but he'd been a boy then. And Tuck, honest, reliable, faithful Tuck. Her companion through the boredom of being ward to Abbot Hugo, confined to the care of his brother, the Sheriff of Nottingham, long before Robin of Loxley had...

Marion dropped her gaze to her hands. One of which, was held by another Robin now. She raised her eyes back to Will.

He was one of the first to fall when she...

Marion swallowed, trying to blank out the images of the past that swam though her head, blotting out the singing of the birds above and the comforting babble of the fire. 'Herne's warning was an old one. At first, I thought I'd heard wrong, because... because she's dead.'

'Who's dead? Will leant towards Marion, his usual impatience tempered by anxiety. 'What did Herne say that we've heard before?

'These were Herne's exact words.' She wiped a hand over her dry lips. 'Only you, Marion of Sherwood, Marion of Leaford, can prevent the power that seeks to shatter the bolts against the evil one.'

Instant chaos broke out amongst the outlaws. Robin watched in stunned silence as his men jumped to their feet, their drawn weapons held out before them, ready to tackle an invisible enemy as Will and John uttered a name they hoped they'd never hear again.

'Morgwyn of Ravenscar!'

Nasir swept both his swords around the camp as he always did when indicating they should begin a search. 'If she is here, we'll find her.'

'Stop!' Robin's voice rang across the clearing. 'You're acting like frightened rabbits! We haven't heard all of Herne's warning yet.' He lowered his voice as he asked Marion, 'Who is this Morgwyn of Ravenscar?'

'A sorceress. We fought her before... umm...'

Robin immediately understood Marion's reticence and smiled, giving her palm a kiss. 'Before me, you mean? No wonder you've been afraid to say. You thought you might hurt my feelings?'

'Yes. I'm sorry...' Marion shrugged helplessly at her friends, who'd re-joined them by the fire. Their ale abandoned, each man cast regular fleeting glances into the growing grey shadows that filled the gaps between the trees.

Speaking more to Marion than the others, Robin smiled, 'I came here, to you all, because I was needed. Your lives before me, and all the good you did back then, should not be forgotten.'

Nasir flicked an eye upwards to check the branches before breaking the uneasy silence that had fallen between them. 'Nothing ever is, Robin.'

Coming to Marion's side, Tuck patted her arm. 'Go on Little Flower. Tell us the rest of Herne's message.'

Grateful for Tuck's solid presence, Marion began again. 'Like I said, Herne showed me a vision. I've been trying to remember every part of it, but it's hard. The heat and the smell of the potion made my head thud.'

'It always does that to me too.' Robin's smile was encouraging. 'Go on.'

'Herne said that only I could prevent those who seek to tear the heart from the forest and pluck the little flower...' Marion reached out and took Tuck's hand in her free palm. 'He said, "We are three but weakness comes...save the woman..." That's when the vision came, beginning with the novice we saw in the village. Abertha, Oswald called her. She was smiling and then falling as if someone had hit her. But then she was smiling again. For a while I felt as though I was all alone, the only person in the forest... Then there was fire and falling antlers and...'

Marion stopped. Her mouth had gone stone dry. She looked again at the hand that belonged to the son of the earl of Huntingdon. Robert of Huntingdon had given up lands, riches and status to become Robin Hood. Marion had always known he'd done it for her. She's always known he loved her - and she had grown to love him. And now she was going to hurt him. She had no choice.

'And?' Robin coaxed.

'And then everyone, except you and me Robin, was stood right here, just as they are now, but ...' Marion's eyes met John's as she silently pleaded with him to help her...to understand. 'But they weren't alone, they were with...'

Foreboding ran up Robin's spine. 'Who, Marion? Who were they with?'

'Robin of Loxley.'

***

'Interesting, don't you think, sister?' Morgwyn stroked the quill's black feathers through her fingers as she looked up from the clay pot.

Rhawn gave a harsh bark of laughter. 'Did you see how fast he let go of his woman's hand at the mention of Loxley? And after he'd promised not to as well.'

'Most satisfying.' Morgwyn jammed a commanding finger in Abertha's direction. 'Stir the cauldron more gently now.'

As the newest member of the coven reduced the speed of the twirl of the willow stick through the ink, Morgwyn rubbed her hands in expectation. 'Let's see what the cauldron can tell us about Hood's rabble.'

'Can we use them to further our aim, sister?'

'Maybe...but first we must learn more about them.' Morgwyn gave a single curt clap over the fire. 'Rhawn, Abertha, focus on the ink. We need to go beneath what we can see. Scan the outlaw's most hidden memories... *Venite videte tua timoribus...* Find the thoughts they can't bear to acknowledge they carry with them.'

A broad grin settled on Rhawn's face as the ink swirled in shades of black and grey before her, creating a marbled pattern across its effervescent surface. 'They have suffered much loss, sister.'

'Oh yes, so very much... and there's so much more to come.'

CHAPTER 7

'If she's back, she'll come for us.'

Little John spoke with solid certainty as the outlaws paced the edge of the clearing. They were anxious to act, but had no idea what to do, or where to go to do it.

Nasir tilted his head in the direction of the nearest road. 'We must post guards. I will take the south road.'

'Good idea.' Will hooked a pouch of ale over his shoulder and stuffed some of Oswald's apples in his pockets. 'I'll head to the Newark Road. Much, you come with me. You're bird signals are better than mine if we need to summon help, so you can be our go-between.'

'Right.' Much ran to his store of sling shots and began to fill his pockets.

Watching his men dart around like trapped flies, a dread that Robin didn't understand gnawed at the back of his mind.

'Wait! Who is this woman? Please, all of you, talk to me.'

As soon as his men stopped moving, their state of confusion overtook again. Robin found himself listening to everyone talking at once. Each sentence, hurriedly spoken, was uttered by the bravest people he'd ever known—and yet every word rang with fear.

'How is she alive?'

'Where is she?'

'What's she want this time?'

Marion barely heard them as she stepped further away from Robin. She held up her right hand, glaring at it as if it were diseased. 'You promised not to let go of my hand, Robin. You promised.'

Forgetting the others for a moment, Robin quickly took it back. As he enveloped her slender fingers between his own, he wiped a stray red hair from her forehead. 'I'm sorry. I don't know why I did, it was a shock at hearing... I... I don't know.'

'You'd only just said our past shouldn't be forgotten! Then you let go of me... you promised! You know how hard that was for me to say. I told you how tough it was back then... and then I met you and we were happy. You and me together. And now...'

'I said I was sorry, I...'

A log landed in the middle of the fire with a thud that sent sparks shooting into the sky. Drawing himself up to his full height, his hands on his hips, Tuck shouted across the camp. 'Be quiet everyone! And for pity's sake, sit down.'

As one the outlaws slumped back to the ground. Robin and Marion joined them, sitting next to each other, still holding hands, but more noticeably apart than before.

'That's better.' Tuck cleared his throat. 'Now then, Herne must have had a reason for what he showed Marion. And if the abbess is involved, then we must be on our guard. But we have to stick together.'

Forcing himself to focus on Tuck and not Marion, Robin asked, 'This Morgwyn of Ravenscar is an abbess?'

'Aye.' John nodded into the flames. 'At least, that's what she pretended to be until she revealed herself as a Devil worshipper. She put us in a cage. Tried to sacrifice us to Lucifer.'

Much's eyes darted between his friends as he took over John's tale. 'Then Robin, you know, um, the other one... 'E got bewitched by that Morgwyn. But Herne did something - I don't know what it was because I was under her spell too - we all were. But it saved us...' Much gulped. 'She isn't really back, is she?'

'Nah, we left her for dead.' Will didn't sound as sure as he looked.

'Sorcery! I hate it.' Grimacing with distaste, Robin threw a loose twig into the fire 'I need to know all about this woman. Does she work alone? What does she look like? Where is she from? I must know *everything.*'

Marion dared to meet his eyes. 'Aren't you angry with me, Robin?'

'Of course not. You didn't choose what Herne told you. We really need to be sure it's her though.' Robin tensed as he asked, 'So, this Morgwyn, John, how did you meet her last time?'

'Right lad, yes. So, a man came to Sherwood, Gareth his name was. He was from Uffcombe.'

Robin was puzzled. 'I don't know an Uffcombe.'

'It's a long way from here. We went because Marion knew Gareth of Uffcombe, he'd been steward to her father. Anyway, the villagers there thought devils were stealing their people, but it was her! Morgwyn of Ravenscar. She bewitched people. The Hounds of Lucifer she called them. She wanted to summon the Devil into the world.'

'She nearly did too!' Tuck grimaced in disgust, crossing himself as he remembered the villager's frightened faces.

'This bewitching, how did it work, Tuck?'

'Each 'hound' wore a square of folded parchment around their necks. If it was destroyed it killed them.'

'What was written on it, do you remember?'

'I'll never forget, Robin.' Tuck took a swig of ale as he recalled the terrible curse. 'It was in Latin, the ink thick and black. Just holding it in my hands made me shudder. It said, "We have signed a treaty with death and with Hell we have made a pact."'

Robin thought for a while. 'Her magic is in the words she uses... I see.'

Will jumped to his feet. 'You don't see, Robin! She had an army! Lords, barons, sheriffs, bishops even. A force to bring Satan to power. Important men at her beck and call. If we hadn't gone to help... if Herne hadn't...' Scarlet's words trailed off as he sank back to the floor, raking his hands through his hair in frustration, mumbling to himself, '...we wouldn't be here, that's all.'

'Was our sheriff one of these hounds?'

'No Robin,' John gave a cheerless laugh. 'Not de Rainault. He hasn't the stomach for that at least.

Will agreed, 'Too much of a coward for a start.'

The wind picked up around them, coiling through the trees as John spoke into the flames, caught in an unwanted memory. 'Morgwyn bewitched us all, Robin. We had no control over what we did. We didn't even know who we were.'

An uneasy silence descended as each outlaw reflected on a time they'd rather forget. Eventually, Tuck brought them back to the present.

'Marion, when Herne said, "a little flower to be plucked", do you think he meant you?'

'It felt like it, but I can't be sure. He said I was the only one who could stop it. But stop what exactly? And how?'

Thinking fast, Robin silently observed his men, as Nasir took over questioning Marion.

'The novice in the vision was the novice in the village?'

'I'm certain it was. Yes.'

Nasir carved a line in the earth with his dagger. 'But you did not say to follow after you saw it was her?'

'No, I...' Marion sat up. 'I didn't, did I.' She pressed a hand against her aching head. 'I don't know why I didn't. I...'

'But I do. I know why.'

A shadow fell across the camp as Robin got to his feet. He felt nausea rise in his stomach as the reason for Marion's unwillingness to share her vision came into startlingly focus. Hoping he was wrong, but convinced he was right, Robin let go of her hand and stepped away from the woman he loved.

Marion reached out for him, but he shook his head and took another step away.

'Pass me Albion, John.'

Reluctantly John passed his friend his sword. 'Why? Where are you going?'

Determined to keep his face impassive, Robin looked at Marion, his voice battling not to sound chocked. 'You didn't ask us to follow Abertha, for the same reason you didn't tell us about Herne's message before now.'

'Robin?' Panic took hold of Marion as she waited to hear him speak the words she'd dreaded hearing.

'You don't want to interfere with the prophecy, do you? If you stop it, then Loxley won't appear. And you *want* to see him. Don't you Marion?

'No, I...'

Robin cut across her, swinging around to face his men, his expression closed. 'You all want to see him. I should leave.'

Will's ever ready anger boiled over as he Robin started to walk away. 'You can't leave. Not now! This is sorcery. You know what that does to your 'ead!'

Without looking back, Robin called out, 'I know that better than anyone, Will. I also know that I was never *ever* meant to meet Robin of Loxley.'

John gripped his quarter staff, not sure if he should go after Robin or stay where he was. 'But it was just a memory, Robin! A warning from Herne.'

As the Hooded Man disappeared into the shadows of the forest, the stunned outlaws turned to Marion of Sherwood, sat on the ground, cradling her arms around herself. Fear pulsed through her as she whispered, 'Robin.'

CHAPTER 8

Nasir fetched two whetstones from their hiding place and passed one to Will. The Saracen's swords didn't need their blades sharpening, but he needed to do something, and preparing for battle was all he could think of.

Marion continued to stare at the place where Robert of Huntingdon had stood only moments before. 'Where do you think he's gone, John?'

'I don't know lass. Give him time to think. He'll calm down.'

'Surely he can't be jealous of my past after all this time?'

John's left eyebrow rose as Will caught his eye. They knew Robin had never come to terms with Marion's previous love for Loxley. 'Don't ask me, lass. He never talks about it.'

Scraping a curved blade across the whetstone, Nasir spoke bluntly. 'We had a life before him. He feels shut out.'

Marion soft voice wavered, 'I know. I just wish...'

Will slipped an arm around her shoulder. 'Wishing won't change anything. Believe me, I've tried.'

Giving Scarlett a brave smile, Marion said, 'Perhaps I shouldn't have told him that I saw Robin.'

'You had no choice, Little Flower.' Tuck peeped up from where he was stashing food into a sack, ready for any emergency journey they may have to make.

'Umm.' Marion hand smoothed over the ground where Robin had been sat only moments ago. 'There was something else, something I didn't get a chance to tell him.'

'How much worse can it get?' Will lifted his newly polished sword blade to the light to examine the tip.

Marion swallowed. 'Herne called me wife of Loxley.'

The outlaws stopped what they were doing and gathered back around her.

John frowned. 'Like Herne was stuck in the past you mean?'

'Of course! That must be it. Thank you, John.' Relief flooded Marion as she regarded her friends. 'I knew he wasn't right. It's so obvious now you've said that!'

'Err, what is?' Much asked.

'What if Morgwyn's got to Herne somehow? What if she's trapped his mind in the past? What if he's forgotten who his son is? Who his son is now, I mean?'

John kneaded his beard thoughtfully. 'That's a lot of what ifs lass.'

'I know, but...'

Will interrupted. 'Hang on a minute. We left Morgwyn for dead. We saw her, lying in the shallows of the water, so are we sure this is her doing?'

'If it isn't, then it's someone who knows a lot about her.' Marion pulled her cloak tighter around her shoulders.' Let's go back to the village and find Oswald. He knew Abertha, the novice from the vision. The only thing that did feel right about what Herne said was that we must save the woman.'

'Good idea, lass.' John picked up his quarterstaff and caught a water pouch as Tuck threw one to each of them. 'Better than just sitting here doing nothing. Douse the fire, Much.'

'Hang on.' Will glanced back to where Robin had been. 'One of us should stay in case he comes back.'

As one, the outlaws looked at Tuck.

'Oh all right then, I'll stay. But don't be long. God knows what you'll find out there.'

***

The ink belched above the fire as Abertha continued to stir it, uncaring that her previously white habit was covered in soot.

Rhawn watched as the picture in the liquid was obscured by the burst of a scolding black bubble, only to clear to show the movement of someone walking through trees. Every now and then, she could see the flash of a man's back as Marion looked towards one of her fellow outlaws.

'Late for an evening walk, but still they walk this way. Do we take our chance to end Marion of Sherwood tonight?'

'And lose our eyes! No Rhawn!' Morgwyn snapped. 'Stir the ink a little faster now Abertha. Feel its power in your veins.'

'Yes, my Lady.'

Morgwyn shone with the expectation of success as she laid a bony hand upon the girl's forehead. 'Your mind is untainted by expectation. It must be you who searches inside their souls, Abertha. We need a face from their past to haunt them. Go deep into each man, one at a time. Show us what you see.'

Beneath Morgwyn's cold palm, sweat broke out on Abertha's brow. The willow remained steady in her hand, but the ink flung itself around the clay bowl, it's movement at odds with the steady stirring, as if the substance itself was trying to speak.

Leaning over the pot, her face consumed with the smoke and vapour that rose from it, making everything in the cottage, except for Morgwyn's bone dry hand, clammy, Abertha murmured words that came directly from her mistress's soul. '*Ostende mihi... Show me... Ostende mihi...*'

Picking up the quill with her free hand, Morgwyn prompted the novice. 'Hunt for a weakness in the men. A wife, a sister, a lover.'

Eventually, Abertha spoke through clenched teeth, her words rising above the gulping chatter of the ink. 'The youngest man, there's someone... Kate... There's pain. He lost her.'

Tutting, her impatience growing, Morgwyn snapped, 'Yes, I can feel that anyway! There's not enough resentment. The hate inside him isn't strong enough. We need more. The quill grows hungry.'

Rhawn saw the quill jerk impatiently in her sister's hand, as if it had a life force of its own. 'What else do you see, Abertha? Work faster!'

The novice's mind roamed from man to man, a brusque shake of her head revealing nothing stronger than the previously dismissed boy's regret and guilt, until she discovered what her mistress was hoping for.

'That one...' She jabbed the willow at the reflection of a man's broad, leather covered, back. 'He has a past. So much death, an engrained sadness never addressed. Scathlock... No, Scarlet. They call him that now, and with good reason.'

Morgwyn pressed her hand harder against Abertha's forehead. 'Yes... I can feel it too. A woman. Taken long past. Never forgotten.'

'Elana.'

As Abertha spoke the name, the flames beneath the cauldron soared higher, and the ink spurted in hot bursts.

Morgwyn's cruel smile returned to her face. 'The ink agrees... It's time to bring forth this Elana.' She paused, her smile widening. 'Or should I say, bring her forth again.'

'What do you mean, *again*?' Rhawn's eyes widened as she saw her sister's pleasure glow in her grey eyes. 'What will this Elana do, sister?'

31

'Confuse them, even more than I intended it to.' She lowered her palm from Abertha's head, causing the girl to sag back from the fire with an exhausted groan.

'It seems Elana's presence will make them doubt who they fight, as well as to how to fight what is to befall them. Satan has surely bestowed his blessing upon our venture.'

Morgwyn raised her hands, the quill squashed securely between both palms, its tip aiming like a dagger towards the clay bowl as she chanted with brittle determination.

'We are three, but they don't know *which* three. Our strength grows, but we need doubt to mask our plans. Now we'll have more than we could have hoped for. And that doubt will lead to chaos—the perfect fuel for the Cauldron of Lucifer!'

CHAPTER 9

The sun was setting by the time the outlaws reached the outskirts of Ollerton village. Leaves waved overhead as the birds greeted the oncoming night in song. The day had been warm and bright, yet as evening took hold, a frost touched the tips of the branches.

'I wish Robin was here.' Marion whispered to John. 'The air doesn't feel right. There shouldn't be frost in May.'

'Magic does strange things, and...' Little John stopped abruptly, beckoning his colleagues into the shadows. 'Footsteps.' He thought he'd imagined it at first, but a few seconds later, the soft footfall of someone approaching became unmistakable.

'Who's that? Can you see, Nasir?'

'It's a girl. We're too far away.'

Sliding quietly through the trees, they approached the outskirts of the orchard that stood between Ollerton and Rufford Abbey. Much glanced anxiously at Marion. 'Is it her?'

'I don't think so. Not unless she's changed her clothes.'

Will stood as if rooted to the forest floor, before twisting away from the sight of the woman picking apples ahead of them. He swung around so violently that he stumbled on a loose stone. Supporting himself on a tree trunk, breathing deeply, his voice barely registered as he murmured, 'No... It can't be... Not again. Not *him*!'

'Will?' Marion clasped her bow as she saw the colour drained from Scarlet's face.

Forcing himself to look back towards the orchard, Will scrubbed a hand over his eyes before he spoke just one word. 'Elana.'

John and Nasir gaped at Will in horror, as John said, 'But that would mean it's... Oh no, not him... It can't be *him*.'

'Him?' Much peered over Marion's shoulder towards the figure of the girl moving around the orchard. 'But Elana's a girl's name. Hang on, isn't Elana...?'

Will patted Much on the shoulder, finishing the sentence for him. 'My dead wife. Yes. Except it can't be, can it.' Taking reassurance from the anger that was rising fast inside him, Will spat, 'How could he think I'd fall for that trick twice?'

'Hush.' Nasir held a finger to his lips, but it was too late. 'The creature, she sees us... she waves...'

Elana Scathlock smiled at Will as if he were the only other person in the world. She didn't move towards him, but reached out a hand, entreating him with a single finger. 'Come Will... Come to me.'

Marion laid a hand on Scarlet's arm. 'This isn't real. That isn't Elana. We've been here before; you said so yourself. It's an enchantment.'

Elana's likeness pulled an apple from the tree and bit into it, her smile warm, her blonde hair lit as if by a halo of sunshine rather than the unseasonal frost that nipped at the trees. 'Will Scathlock... My William.'

'Gulnar!' Scarlet spoke the name they were all thinking now, each letter lay like bile on his tongue. 'His style ain't it, messing with our minds. It ain't Morgwyn, it's 'im!'

'Will...' Elana walked into the depths of the orchard, the evening shadows slowly swallowing her, hiding her from view.

John clutched Will's shoulder. 'She's leaving. Don't follow her, lad.'

'I ain't gonna.'

Watching Will carefully, knowing he was battling a monster none of them could see, Marion muttered, 'What if we're *meant* to follow her, John?'

'No lass, it's a trap.'

Nasir agreed. 'And we don't know who's laid it. Which makes it twice as dangerous.'

Marion's brow crinkled as she thought over everything Herne had said to her. 'I was so sure it was Morgwyn. And Robin, Robin of Loxley I mean, he never even met Gulnar.'

Checking over his shoulder, as if expecting to see Owen of Clun's mad soothsayer appear before them, Much said, 'But what if it is Gulnar? Reading our 'eads like Will said.' He lifted a hand to his chest, remembering the wounds he'd sustained after falling into a foresters trap on their second encounter with the bald-headed sorcerer.

'Or what if it's both of them?' Nasir hissed, 'Herne said three.'

'Oh great!' Will barked under his breath. 'Another one as well! Morgwyn, Gulnar, and the Devil alone knows who else.'

John cursed into the dark as he muttered, 'Quite possibly he does, lad. Quite possibly he does.'

***

Robin hesitated at the mouth of the cave. He could hear the sound of the wind rushing around inside before him, but as he checked over his shoulder into the forest, the atmosphere there remained calm.

Clutching Albion in his hand, Robin stepped through the cavern's narrow mouth. Immediately the temperature dropped. Goose-pimples dotted his skin as he moved forwards. He could see the play of the fire casting shadows against the walls, but its flames were low; ready to die into nothing but embers. The sound of the gale he'd heard from the outside, was just that – a noise. As if that was the only remnant of a storm that had passed through Herne's private domain.

The place was in disarray.

'Herne?' Robin bent to pick up some fallen pottery and placed it on the large altar rock in the centre of the cave. His footsteps echoed as he walked around the vast space. What had happened? It was as if a whirlwind had hit the cave. Two echoing steps later, and Robin dashed forwards. 'Herne!'

For a moment he thought he'd seen his master, but it was just the horned headdress he often wore, discarded to the ground. *Or thrown aside?*

Bending to pick it up, Robin held it close as he surveyed the rest of the cave. 'Marion said she saw fallen antlers in her vision. Herne... can you hear me?'

Laying the antlers on the altar, keeping his hands on the headdress, Robin tried again, 'Father, can you hear me?'

A faint sound, more like a shadow of a noise than a voice, mumbled, 'My son.'

Robin spun round, but there was no one to see as his fists tightened around the antlers. 'Herne, where are you?'

'In the blood and the bone...hidden from Lucifer's Lady.'

'Lucifer's Lady? Is that this Morgwyn of Ravenscar that everyone is terrified of?'

'You are Herne's Son. You are the past, present, future...'

'That doesn't answer my question. What must I do?'

The spirit's voice weakened, as if Herne were labouring for breath. 'Find your woman. Save her.'

'Marion?' Robin's pulse raced and his head began to ache as he spoke into the lifeless eyes before him, 'Save Marion and not the nun?'

'Marion.'

The Hooded Man dropped the stag's head to the altar and ran to the mouth of the cave. 'I'm a fool! I should have listened to Marion. I should have trusted her... I...'

Herne's voice erupted from its faint murmur. Its volume reached a head-splitting crescendo, filling the cave, shaking through Robin's entire being, each word hitting his heart.

'Save Marion of Loxley.'

CHAPTER 10

Robin staggered away from the cave, his blood pounding in his ears. Instinct told him to go back to the others, to apologise for leaving, and to tell them about the chaos he'd found in Herne's cave. But pride sent him walking in the other direction.

Ducking between some thickly seeded ash trees, Robin crashed to the ground, holding his aching head in his hands.

Marion had a headache when she went to see Herne.

He swigged some water from the pouch at his belt. Its fresh, cool, taste eased the bitter prickle at the back of his throat.

Marion said it was as if Herne wasn't really there. He must have already been fading to wherever he's hiding when he called her.

'How long was I in there?' Robin murmured as he stared up at the night sky. 'It must be nearly midnight.'

Leaning against a tree trunk, he sighed. 'Loxley.'

He had nothing against the first Hooded Man. Nothing at all. He'd been a hero. A good man whom his friends had adored. They would have done anything for him back then, just as they did for him now—but Marion had loved him. She still loved him. And that was the problem. Robin closed his eyes.

How can I ever match up to the ghost of such a man as that? I simply can't— even when, to the eyes of the county at least, I've all but become that man.

He wasn't like Loxley though. He didn't try to be. And whatever doubts he had now, Robert of Huntingdon, Herne's second son, knew instinctively he was right about one thing. It would be a mistake to meet Robin of Loxley, even if the Loxley his friends were sure to see wasn't real.

None of this can be real.

Herne's Son *had* died. No question. If he hadn't, Herne the Hunter would never have summoned another. And yet...

'Save your woman.' Robin mulled the words over in his mind. 'My woman, not *the* woman.'

Robin got to his feet and walked into the furthest depths of Sherwood. He hadn't realised where he was going until he was almost in Ollerton. His head had been too full of the woman he loved and the man she'd loved before him.

As the orchard belonging to Rufford Abbey came into view, Robin stopped and took stock of his surroundings. Nothing stirred. Resting his back against a tree, he stifled a yawn.

Why did I come here? Why did I walk this way?

Robin closed his eyes and tried to think.

Marion said there was something about Herne that wasn't right. She's no fool, she knows her husband died. She knew it would upset me to hear that Loxley might be seen again by the others, and so she tried to protect my feelings.

Shame crept up Robin's spine. Marion and his friends could be in trouble right now. Herne *was* in trouble.

And what did I do? I behaved like a spoilt earl's son and stomped off into the forest.

Shaking his head in self-disgust, Robin stepped back onto the track that would take him home. He'd only gone a couple of paces when he froze. There was a figure ahead of him, wandering through the trees, its outline hazy through the shadows.

'Will? John?' Robin's head was aching harder now. His eyes refused to focus properly as the person got closer. 'Hello?'

Robin pulled Albion from his belt, only to lower it again when he saw a woman on the path before him. She was looking from side to side as if nervously searching for something.

'Who's there?'

'Don't be afraid,' Robin smiled. 'I was searching for a novice that's gone missing.'

Not sure why he'd said that, but knowing that it was probably true and, that if he knew his men and Marion at all, that's what they'd have been doing while he was feeling sorry for himself, Robin felt a memory nudge him. 'Have we met before?'

'I don't think so.' The blonde gave a shy smile as she pulled her cloak around her shoulders.

'What are you doing out in the forest alone?'

A voice in Robin's head started screaming now, telling him he knew this woman and that there was some reason she shouldn't be trusted. But one half of Robin's mind dismissed the other as paranoia.

'I was cold. There's a pile of firewood to the right side of the orchard. I was going to fetch some. Would you help me?'

Returning her increasingly dazzling smile, Robin walked towards her. 'Of course. It's not safe to be out this late on your own.'

Bending to pick up some wood, Robin's eyes kept flicking to the girl. 'Did I see you in the village with Oswald earlier? I'm sure we've met before.'

By way of reply, the girl gestured ahead, to where a wisp of smoke could be seen rising through the trees. 'I live in the hermit's cottage, near the village.'

The throb in Robin's head grew more intense as he remembered what he'd heard about the cottage. 'Oswald said the place was empty.'

The snap of a twig behind Robin broke through the growing fog in his head. He whirled round just in time to see two other women grinning at him. A thick branch was already raised in the hand of one of them and was coming his way.

It landed on his head with a sickening crack, before he'd even registered what was happening. Robin's howl of pain was smothered by Rhawn, who held her cloak firmly over the outlaw's face until he lost consciousness.

Morgwyn tutted. 'Well, wolfshead, Oswald was wrong!'

Rotating sharply on her heels, the sorceress headed back into the hermitage, leaving her fellow witches to drag their visitor's body in after them.

***

The cottage was dominated by the cloying scent and spitting sound of the black ink spluttering in the pot lodged across the cauldron. The longer it boiled, the more it stank of death and decay.

As Rhawn and Abertha manoeuvred the outlaw's senseless body into the confined space, Morgwyn observed the sway of the potion. 'You did well Abertha.'

With a click of her fingers, Morgwyn restored the girls her natural features, the essence of Elana fading as she commanded, 'Come here and keep the ink moving, the quill is nearly ready to write its way into his soul.'

Morgwyn passed the willow back stick to Abertha, before instructing her sister. 'Rhawn, hold him still. Before I take his soul, I want to see what's on the Hooded Man's mind.'

'My pleasure.' Rhawn swung a leg over him, and sat on his chest, her hands running suggestively up and down his arms.

'I meant for you to hold him still, not straddle the man!'

'There is no reason why we should not take pleasure in our work.' Rhawn flicked some blonde hair away from where it had half hidden their captives face. 'I'm simply admiring the view as I assist you.'

With a grunt, Morgwyn pulled her mind from her sister's dubious tastes and spread her palms out before her. Holding the quill high in her right hand she chanted, '*Venite videte tua timoribus.*' Turning the quill, so it looked like an arrow pointing at the outlaw, the sorceress grinned, 'Let's see what's on your mind, boy of Huntingdon.'

The flames behind his captive became blood red as, impatient to know what her sister saw, Rhawn leant forward so her hands could caress their prisoner's chest. 'What have you discovered Morgwyn?'

'Guilt and fear. He's worried about losing Marion and regrets leaving the camp.'

'How sweet.' Rhawn spat out her sarcasm with a twisted smile.

'There's more.' Morgwyn lowered the quill, so its tip almost touched Robin's forehead. 'He feels bad for letting down his men and guilt about abandoning his future earldom...'

She paused, screwing her eyes shut as she drove on into the hidden recesses of Robin's mind. 'This will be useful to us... he questions the truth of Marion's love. There's so much conflict within him to manipulate there. Then there's that pathetic sheriff, de Rainault and his acolyte, Sir Guy of Gisburne...'

Morgwyn gave a gasp of pleasure, clapping her hands, so the quill quivered in her grasp, its feather bristling in hunger. 'So, the oak had two acorns...'

The sorceress opened her eyes and spoke hurriedly. 'Abertha, Rhawn... evoke the ink. Quickly now, I need to go deeper still. This is a secret he hides even from himself.'

The two younger witches murmured together, their chant filling the cottage. '*Suscipe verba haec tua est vinculum tenebris Dominus.*'

'Keep going sisters, repeat the spell until I say stop.' Morgwyn glared down at the fallen man. 'What is Guy of Gisburne to you Herne's Son?'

She placed her hand on his forehead. 'Tell me your thoughts. Speak to them, to the Lady of the Cauldron with your mind, wolfshead. Who is Gisburne to you?'

Robin's head rocked from side to side as something inside him fought against the chanting.

'Rhawn! Help me. Keep his neck still.'

From her position on Robin's chest, Rhawn's hands clamped themselves against the side of his head, struggling to quieten him as Morgwyn pressed her hand harder against his forehead.

Touching the quill to his temples, Morgwyn demanded, 'Tell me! *Venite videte tua timoribus.*'

The word, 'enemy', escaped through Robin's tight lips, but it wasn't enough for Morgwyn.

'Somehow he's fighting me. Herne must have done something. There's a fog inside his mind that I didn't put there.'

'Perhaps Herne is protecting his son from your magic?'

Morgwyn ignored Rhawn as she drew a line with the un-inked pen across the outlaw's face. 'There is more...tell me more!'

'No! I...'

The quill rested on Robin's cheek. Morgwyn pushed it so hard against his flesh that a dot of blood appeared, making the outlaw cry out even from the depths of his enchantment.

'Tell me who Guy of Gisburne is to you!'

'MY FATHER'S SON!'

Robin's head lolled to the side, exhausted by the battle with his own conscience.

Morgwyn sat back on her haunches. Her face glowed in the orange fire light, 'Finally! I have found the chaos we need. Roll up his sleeve, Rhawn.'

'Can't I open his tunic instead?'

'Do as I say!' Morgwyn scowled at her sister as she threw a further command to the newest member of their coven. 'Abertha, fill the quill.'

The enslaved novice obeyed with swift obedience, her eyes never once leaving the outlaw as she stirred the pot.

Morgwyn, her ink filled weapon to hand, paused, wanting to savour the moment. Then, pressing the quill hard against his flesh, she began to write on the Hooded Man's arm with the hot black ink.

A single cry of 'No!' shot from Robin's lips, but no more words came as the outlaw lay, suddenly lifeless, on the dusty floor of the hermit's cottage.

Watching the words sink into his flesh, Morgwyn placed the quill back on the table and smiled.

'It is done. He is ours now.'

CHAPTER 11

The outlaws had gathered blearily together around the fire at first light. None of them had slept much, but no one mentioned it. Each had been caught in memories of a time before Robert of Huntingdon had found them. A time before Loxley's death at the hands of the sheriff's men.

After taking some food from Tuck, they'd split into three groups; Will and Much heading to the south of the forest, John and Nasir to the north, while Marion and Tuck waited at the camp, hoping Robin would come back while the others hunted for him.

Now they were alone, Marion huddled next to the friar and looked up through the trees at the pale blue sky. It would be hot later, but for now a cool haze hung across the canopy, making her shiver.

'The thing is Tuck, I never was Marion Loxley. I've never even been to Loxley. I was Marion of Sherwood when I got married. If Robin had just stopped to think before he marched off, then...'

'He will. He just needs to calm down. He'll be back as soon as he realises he's been hasty.' Tuck patted Marion's shoulder as she rested against his side.

'But what if it is Gulnar, Tuck? I can't face him again. Remember what happened last time—and the time before that. He nearly destroyed us.'

Marion saw the fallen body of Robert of Huntingdon rear up in her mind. At the time, she hadn't known what she'd seen was no more than a clay golem Gulnar had created to fool them into thinking their leader was dead. It had felt real to her as she'd stood over the broken body of Herne's second son, and her heart had broken all over again.

Screwing her eyes shut, a hopeless shield against an image that had never truly left her, Marion turned to her friend. 'I can't face it again, Tuck. I can't!

Robin must know I love him. That's why I went away, why I joined Abbess Constance *and* why I came back.'

'I know Little Flower.'

'And as for Robin, he almost...'

Marion's sentence trailed into thin air as the sound of footsteps made her and Tuck spin around.

'I almost what, Marion?'

'Robin! I've been so worried. The others are out searching Sherwood for you.'

With a nod to Tuck, Robin sat next to Marion and took her hands. 'I'm sorry. I behaved like a child. Will you forgive me?'

'I expect so.'

Conscious of being in the way, Tuck clambered to his feet with a puffing grunt. 'I'll get cooking then. That lot will be hungry when they get back.' The friar brushed his hand together. 'They are *always* hungry.'

'Thanks Tuck.' Robin pulled Marion to his side, stroking her hair as it brushed against him. 'I went to find Herne. His cave looks like it's been hit by a whirlwind. He wasn't there. His antlers were on the floor.'

Marion shuddered against his shoulder. 'Like in my vision.'

Robin scratched at his arm. 'Yes. I'm sorry I doubted you, even for a second.'

'It must have been a shock, hearing about Loxley.' Marion paused, 'we wondered if Herne had been trapped in the past someone. It was as if...' Marion broke off as Robin rubbed his arm harder through the fabric of his tunic. 'Are you alright?'

'My arm's itching a bit. I must have caught it on a tree or bramble or something.'

Marion lifted a hand to his face and ran a fingertip over the tiny scar on his cheek. 'Whatever it was got you here too. Do you want me to have a look at your arm?'

Robin rapidly snatched it away, before shrugging the gesture off with a smile. 'It's nothing. I was careless in my haste to get back to apologise and tell you why I was such a...'

She pushed a strand of blonde hair behind his ear as he tried to find the right words. 'Such a...?'

'A fool. I'm a jealous fool.'

Marion smiled into his eyes as Robin's hands entwined with hers. 'You're my fool, and I'm glad you're back.'

Their kiss lasted so long that Tuck was obliged to spend extra time rearranging the items in the hollowed-out tree trunk they used as a food store, and then found himself planning supper for the next three nights.

***

'He hides his new allegiance well.' Morgwyn added a second vial of ink to the cauldron's clay pot. As Abertha stirred, the dark blue shade of the new liquid swirled and fizzed against the molten mixture already within. 'The Hooded Man's woman is beautifully blind to the situation.'

Rhawn cackled, 'While the Hooded Man himself is just plain beautiful. Can I keep him to play with afterwards?'

'You can do whatever you want with him, just don't do it anywhere near me,' Morgwyn tutted at her sister before turning to Abertha. 'Give the willow stick to Rhawn. She will stir for a while.'

As Abertha obeyed, Morgwyn picked a bottle made of blue glass from the table next to the cauldron and poured the contents into a cup.

'Drink this. You're going for a walk into Sherwood. This...' She lifted the clear liquid over the cauldron, silently cursing it, before passing it to Abertha, '...will make sure you reach your destination correctly attired.'

CHAPTER 12

Tuck passed two pieces of bread to the couple sat together by the fire. It lightened his heart to have Robin back and Marion looking so relieved. Yet, as he carried on with his cooking, he sensed a shadow hanging over them. Listening carefully to the conversation by the fire, Tuck wished the others would hurry up and return to the camp.

'Did you go and look for the novice, Marion?' Crumbs sprinkled over his clothes as Robin chewed his bread.

'We did, but we found someone else on the way. Someone we shouldn't have been able to find.'

'Who?'

Marion glimpsed in Tuck's direction. Encouraged by the friar's silent dip of encouragement, she described their walk towards Ollerton, and how a girl, who'd been made to look like Elana Scathlock, had stood in the orchard.

'It was like Cromm Cruac, the village of the dead Gulnar tried to trap us in, all over again.'

'Gulnar!?' Robin tore a chunk off the end of his bread and watched as more crumbs scattered to the ground. 'But we finished him Marion, you know we did. He couldn't have survived.'

'Just as I was sure Morgwyn of Ravenscar was left for dead.'

Silence hung between them for a moment before Robin asked, 'Will didn't think it really was Elana this time, did he?'

'No. But he's worried... we all are. What if this isn't Morgwyn, what if it's Gulnar playing with our heads, or worse? What if...'

'If it's both of them?' Robin echoed the outlaw's earlier fears before taking a long drink of water.

45

'Or it could be Morgwyn interfering with our minds just as we first thought. We didn't see her die, just her body on the ground. If we were wrong and she lived...'

Robin closed his eyes. His head was aching again as he struggled to make sense of what Marion had been saying to him, while puzzling together Herne's warnings. 'Herne spoke to me through the antlers. It was like he was there in soul but not body. He said I was the past, present and future. I think he's put himself somewhere so he can hide from her.'

'So you think this *is* Morgwyn and not Gulnar?' Marion's relief was short lived, unsure which nightmare she'd rather live through again. 'Herne certainly made me think it was her. And if Morgwyn is affecting Herne somehow, then maybe she's altered his prophecies. So, how can we know which parts of his message to trust?'

'I don't know. Scarlet was right, magic messes with your head.' Robin jumped up. 'I want to take you somewhere safe until this is over. Will you let me? Please.'

Staying where she was, Marion hesitated, 'But, I can help you. We work best together, we always have. If we just wait for the others...'

Taking hold of both her hands, Robin held her gaze, pleading with her to understand. 'Look what sorcery did to us last time! I couldn't bear it if...'

'You're sending me back to Halstead!' Marion was horrified as she broke from the hold of Robin's eyes, looking instead at Tuck's reassuringly stout back. She could see his herb filled hands hovering above the cooking pot, and knew he was listening to what was going on behind him.

Robin shook his head. 'Of course not. I'd never send you away for good. But if you went somewhere safe, somewhere you could come and go as you pleased until this was over... how about the hermit's cottage that Oswald mentioned?'

Tuck's eyes met Marion's for a fleeting second before he joined them. 'You'd be close to the monks there I suppose. Not a bad place to avoid sorcery.'

Marion was surprised. 'You think I should go, Tuck? It's not that far from where we saw Elana.'

Robin smiled reassuringly as he pulled her to her feet. 'You could have been anywhere when you were sent that vision to haunt Will. She wants to spook us.'

'It's working!'

Sending up a prayer for Will, John, Nasir and Much to hurry up, Tuck nodded, 'I think, if you're the one who's supposed to stop whatever's happening Little Flower, then you're better off safe so you can think what to do, while we get on with finding out exactly who it is we're up against. Plus, you could visit the abbey to find out more about Abertha from her uncle.'

'I suppose so.'

Robin slapped Tuck on the back in thanks. 'We'll go now. Oswald said the place was empty. I'm sure no one would mind.'

***

Marion paused as the track way through the forest gave them the chance to branch off to the right, towards Ollerton, or straight on to the orchard and the hermit's cottage beyond.

'Don't you think we should ask Oswald if it's alright first?'

'It's the monks we should ask really, Marion, and as they have left the place abandoned for ages, I'm sure they won't mind. They're unlikely to even notice.' Robin used the end of his bow to indicate the way along the forward path. Two steps later, and they could just see the roof of the cottage on the other side of the orchard. 'Let me get you safely inside, but then I'll go and talk to Oswald if it makes you feel better. He's always been so kind to us.'

Following Robin, Marion peered into the trees to either side of them. 'I still wish we'd had time to tell the others.'

Robin scratched at his arm as he stooped under a low hanging branch. 'Tuck will tell them.'

'Are you sure that arm's alright?'

'Yes, it's fine.' Robin pointed through a patch of fledgling oak trees to the back of the cottage. 'Here we are. It won't be for long I'm sure.'

'I suppose...' Marion stopped walking as an icy chill shot down her back.

'Why have you stopped?' Robin turned, holding out his hand for her to take,

Marion shook her head, moving backwards.

'Something's wrong, can't you feel it?'

Robin pulled his sword and searched through the saplings, but his smile remained. 'Your imagination is getting the better of you. It's fine.'

Taking a reluctant step closer to him, Marion stopped again and sniffed. 'I thought this place was abandoned. I can smell wood smoke.'

'So can I.' This time Robin frowned, holding her hand as they edged forward more carefully. 'Maybe Oswald was mistaken about the place being empty.'

At the door, Robin reached out with Albion, and touched the tip of the sword against the wood, using the blade to push it open. Gingerly, he stepped forward and peeped inside. 'There's been a fire recently, but it is empty now. Come on.'

Still cautious, Marion followed Robin into the dim, cramped space. The aroma of wood smoke was strong, but there was no sign of life as she unhooked her bow from her shoulder, so she could fit through the door.

No sooner were they both inside, than the door slammed shut, trapping them within, and a face Marion recognised with nauseating clarity emerged from the shadows.

'How lovely. It's so rare we have visitors. Rhawn, seize her! Seize Marion of Sherwood!'

'It *is* you!' Marion froze for a split second, before whirling round in terror. 'Run Robin... it's her! It's Morgwyn, it's... Oomph....'

A gnarled hand covered Marion's mouth. It tasted like charred wood and stank of rotting food as Marion squirmed beneath it.

'So this is the Hooded Man's woman, sister.'

'It is.'

Rhawn pulled Marion's head back, so she could see into her frightened eyes. 'He's far too pretty for you girl.'

Robin dived forward to pull Marion free, but a wave of Morgwyn's hands and his arms hung limp at his sides.

'Stay still Herne's Son.'

'Robin!' Muffled by the stinking palm, Marion bit into Rhawn's meagre flesh, causing the witch to drop her with a cursed bawl of outraged pain. Angry tears heated Marion's face as her arms were wrenched up behind her back. 'No. It can't happen again. It can't!'

'Tears? How quaint.' The sorceress laughed as she addressed the vacant man near the door of the cottage. 'Go into the forest. You have work to do, Herne's Son.'

The order woke him from his frozen state. 'Yes, my Lady.'

Marion watched in dismay as the man she loved made for the door. 'Robin, come back! It isn't real... it's Morgwyn she's...'

Rhawn threw a hand back over Marion's mouth. 'Don't you dare bite me again!'

Morgwyn laughed softly, running a jagged fingernail over Marion's cheek. 'Save your breath woman!'

Taking no notice, Marion kicked out as Rhawn half dragged, half pushed, her towards the cauldron. She yelled through the witch's dirty fingers. 'Let me go... he'll fight you... he'll...'

'No!' Morgwyn clapped her hands hard in front of Marion's face, silencing her tongue with a snakelike smile. 'He won't. He'll do what he's told.'

***

'Thank goodness you lot are back.' Tuck threw down his wooden spoon as Will and Much appeared from the cover of the forest, with John and Nasir only seconds behind them. 'Robin's been here.'

'Here?' Will took a swig from the ale pouch Tuck passed him. 'Oh great, so while we've been searching the forest, he's been warming himself by the fire all day!'

John's eyes narrowed, 'So, where is he? And where's Marion?'

'Robin took her to the hermit's cottage near Ollerton. He wanted her safe and out of harm's way while we sorted out whatever's happening.'

Will jumped back to his feet, his face red. 'What? Are you serious, Tuck!? And you let them go?'

'Well, yes. Surely with Oswald so close and the monks on the doorstep Marion would be safe there. Herne told Robin that Marion was the one we needed to protect, not the nun so...' Tuck's words faded as he saw the panic etched on his friend's faces. 'What is it?'

'But Tuck, that's where we saw... where the woman that looked like... like Elana was... near the hermit's cottage.'

'But you said you saw her on the other side of the orchard, that's not that near... is it?'

'Oh Tuck!' John groaned as Tuck regarded his friend's in dismay.

'But that image of Elana could have been conjured anywhere couldn't it... I mean... It wasn't just because of the cottage being quite near and... You don't think that Robin...' Tuck stammered, unable to finish his sentence, 'Do you, John?'

'Robin wasn't with us when we went there. He doesn't know where exactly we saw Elana.'

'But he *does*.' Tuck loosen the clasp of his cloak at his throat, 'Marion told him. And Marion knew.'

Much forced a smile, 'But Tuck's right. It must be safe. That Elana came there because that's where *we* were, and we didn't go into the cottage did we? We were on the other side of the orchard. Robin would never take Marion somewhere dangerous, and Oswald did say it was empty.'

The outlaws stared at each other, as Nasir hissed, 'No. It felt wrong there. We must go. Now.'

'If anything has happened to her, I'd never forgive myself.' Tuck ran to the food store. 'Much, damp down the fire. I'll pour some stew into some cups. We can eat as we go. I'm coming with you this time.'

'Good idea.' John lifted his quarter staff back up as an unseasonably cold breeze shook the tree canopy above them. 'What was that?'

'What?' Will copied John and looking towards the woods to the south of the camp. 'I can't see anything.'

'Shush, lad, listen.' John held a finger to his lips as he breathed, 'Someone's coming.'

The pottery beaker Tuck had been holding slipped from his hand and smashed to pieces as it hit the side of the cooking pot. Crossing himself, the friar stepped nearer his friends.

They'd all pulled their weapons, but not one of them had raised them ready to strike.

Much was the first to speak. His shock muted voice seemed uncommonly loud across the clearing. 'That's my... brother.'

Little John caught Scarlet's eye. 'He isn't real. Remember Elana.'

Taking a cautious step towards their unspeaking visitor, Will muttered, 'Loxley?'

Herne's first son said nothing as Nasir crept to Will's side. '*La ymkn 'an yakun.*'

'What?' Will hissed.

'I said, it can't be.'

'And yet he's there, Nasir.'

Tuck crossed himself again as Loxley walked towards them, just as he'd always done. His face set in determination, but his smile welcoming.

'Little Flower was right. She really did see Robin of Loxley, and now we can see him too. *Exactly* as she said she would.'

CHAPTER 13

Rhawn screwed a handful of Marion's hair up in her fist and tugged, leaving her prisoner with no choice but to peer into the pulsating cauldron ink.

'Robin of Loxley.'

She gasped out the words as the heat from the potion seared the side of her face, making her eyes water. Despite Herne's warning, it was still a shock to see him there, in the forest with her friends.

Her voice honeysweet, Morgwyn asked, 'Aren't you pleased you're husband's back?'

'It isn't him... it *isn't* him.'

Rhawn shoved Marion to the side so she could leer at the reflection of Loxley. 'Another pretty boy. You have all the luck, Marion of Leaford.'

'Sister!' Morgwyn glared at Rhawn. 'Stir the ink. It's time we summoned Abertha home.'

Dragged, so that she was half stood, half crouched at Rhawn's side, Marion choked against the heat. 'Abertha? The novice from Ollerton? What have you done with her?'

Morgwyn laughed in mock pity. 'Herne is dying, your friends are lost to their grief and Robin Hood is under my control, and yet you worry about a miserable would-be nun. How gut wrenchingly sweet.'

Marion squirmed helplessly in Rhawn's hand, making Morgwyn laugh anew. 'I wonder what your friends will do now. Fascinating isn't it.'

As her fire-sore eyes streamed with tears of grief for her lost husband and concern for the man she loved, Marion mumbled, 'Oh, Robin.'

Barking with glee, Morgwyn nudged her sister. 'Listen to her, Rhawn. The pathetic creature doesn't even know which Hooded Man she's pleading for.'

With a precise clap of her hands, the sorceress' mockery morphed into a command. 'A change of scene, I think. Let's see what Herne's other son is up to. Stir in the opposite direction Rhawn.'

Marion fought to twist away from the simmering ink as Morgwyn ran her hands over the side of the cauldron, her hands magically unaffected by the searing heat. 'You can't win woman. Look into the cauldron.'

She clapped again, her held arms high as she raised her voice to the Devil she worshipped. 'Satan, Beelzebub, Lord of Darkness, help us show Marion of Sherwood, Marion of Leaford, Marion Loxley, what the Hooded Man has become.'

Unable to tear her eyes from the vision appearing between the swirls of smoke, Marion trembled as she witnessed Robin walking through the forest, his hood pulled up over his blonde hair.

Morgwyn examined the ink closely, wallowing in her coming victory. 'Herne is hiding from his son. You, his woman, have been taken from him... that just leaves the final corner of the triangle to be removed. Then no Hooded Man will ever interfere with my plans again.'

Marion's remaining strength weakened as, with despair gnawing at her, she saw Robin Hood pick a flint from his pocket and bend to some twigs on the forest floor.

Rhawn chuckled. 'Resourceful, that wolfshead. He's already found the means to start a fire.'

'Even though he doesn't need them.' Morgwyn clicked her fingers and the sticks Robin held burst into flames. 'What do you think Lady Marion, will the torch he holds be enough to keep him warm, or do you think a bigger blaze is required? An inferno perhaps?'

'Sherwood?' Marion wasn't sure if the word had left her lips, or if she'd just thought it. The image of burning trees she'd seen in Herne's cave imprinted itself on the forefront of her mind.

Rhawn laughed again as her sister chanted into the clay pot, making the ink jump with the rhythm of a heart beating.

'*Adolebitque silvam!*'

Time seemed to slow down as, her eyes wide with dread, Marion witnessed Robin Hood - Herne's Son, sworn protector of Sherwood and its people - throw the flaming branches to the ground.

'NO! Robin, don't!'

Morgwyn threw her head back, screeching her joy. 'The forest burns! Hail Lucifer!'

As Rhawn joined in Morgwyn's chant to their dark lord and master,

Marion's tears dropped uselessly into the ink, sizzling against its demonic surface. 'Robin! Oh Robin, what have you done?'

Suddenly Morgwyn broke off her cackle and shot out a hand. Squeezing Marion's chin, her bony fingers dug into the pale freckled skin as she taunted, 'And the Hooded Man shall come to the forest...and burn it to the ground!'

CHAPTER 14

'No one go near him.'

Will continued to gawp at Robin of Loxley as if he was seeing a ghost. Perhaps he was... and yet the man he saw before him felt so real.

Much shuffled to Scarlet's side, desperate to greet their visitor, but too afraid to move. 'But he's my brother. You are, aren't you, Robin? You're really my brother?'

The desperation in Much's voice was heart-breaking.

As he took a tentative step nearer to Loxley, Tuck barred his way. 'He isn't speaking, Much. If that really were your brother, he'd have hugged you by now. He'd have explained himself straight away and asked us where Marion is, but he's just standing there.'

John rested a hand on Much's shoulder. 'Tuck's right lad, that isn't him. Marion saw this. She told us it would happen. Herne was warning us.'

'That's right. *Of course*!' Tuck tore his eyes away from the vision of Loxley and turned to John. 'Past, present and future! That's the three Herne meant, not three people! Forget Gulnar and any other nightmares from our past. There's just one monster here, and that's the Lady of the Cauldron!'

Little John's eyes never left Loxley. He could feel the lure. The vision of the man they'd known wanted them to come forward. John had the strangest notion that he'd only come properly to life if they touched him. The giant grimaced at the thought. 'What are you talking about, Tuck?

'When Robin was here, he said Herne had tried to reach him. That he'd warned him about the past present and future. He must have meant Robin of Loxley, Robert of Huntingdon and...'

John and Will spoke at the same time, neither wanting to believe what they were saying. 'The Hooded Man that comes next!'

'This is bad.' Will took a step back, gesturing for the others to do the same. 'I wish Loxley'd move or do something. E's giving me the creeps.'

'He is waiting for something.' Nasir drew his swords, crossing them protectively across his chest. 'Something is wrong.'

'Tell us something we don't know!'

'No Will, something else. There is smoke.' Nasir waved a sword to a place beyond where Loxley hovered. 'Come.'

Nasir was already running, skirting past an immobile Loxley as Much sniffed the air. 'What smoke?'

'Don't touch him as you pass!' John called as they chased after Nasir, trusting the Saracen's instincts even though he wasn't sure he couldn't trust his own.

Dragging Tuck after him, helping the friar to keep up with the others, Much shouted, 'What about *that* Robin? We can't just leave him.'

Panting with each step, Tuck shot his friend a kind smile. 'Let's worry about the living first, Much.'

John careered to a halt behind Nasir, who had paused, trying to work out the best way to run. 'I can smell smoke too now. That's not a poacher's fire that's... *FIRE!* Look! It's Sherwood!'

Sprinting now, with Tuck coming up behind them, the outlaws found themselves facing a wall of flame. Not a bird sang as a large circle of ash trees blackened before their eyes, sending dust and smoke into the air, choking the immediate atmosphere. At the base of the trees, yellow and orange flames wove like snakes around their trunks, travelling along their raised roots and devouring any ground coverage in its path.

'How did this happen?' Scarlet's jaw dropped as trees blazed like gigantic torches in the darkening night.

Nasir shrugged. 'Questions later. We need to stop it spreading.'

Beyond the ash trees, the fire had been slower to take hold. Throwing off his jerkin, John smothered the flames at his feet as they tried to eat up a nearby clump of forest flowers. He shouted over the hungry roar. 'I'll take this bit. It's no good fighting the main fire, but if we can stop it spreading, then maybe... Will can you get closer?'

Scarlet held his hand over his eyes against the glare of the fires heat. 'We need water! Much! Run back to the camp, get blankets and buckets.'

'But what if he's still there?'

'He won't be.' Will coughed as the wind blew splinters of chard wood in his direction. 'I reckon he was sent to stop us getting here too fast. Hurry Much!'

Tuck had just swiped his cowl over some newly caught grass at the base of a tree when he spotted a figure out of the corner of his eye.

'It's Robin! Look, over there...' Pointing with one hand to the opposite side of the burning circle trees, Tuck stamped across the fledgling flames.

'It *is* him.' John wiped his brow as he squinted though the trunks. The roar of the flames grew louder as another tree canopy caught light, its leaves fizzling and dropping like an evil autumn. 'Robin!'

Robert of Huntingdon, his tunic in his hands, suddenly looked up from where he was trying to stop the fire from devouring his terrain and bounded towards Little John, his face smeared with soot.

'John! Thank goodness you're all here.' He beat at the flames with his top, while continuing to stomp his boots over as much as the ground as he could. 'Come on Tuck, don't stop! Use your cloak to kill the flames. It's spreading.'

Breathless, Tuck resumed his beating as he shouted over the sound of a falling branch, 'Is Marion safe? We were worried that maybe someone had got to the cottage first. The same someone who made Elana appear perhaps?'

His voice hoarse from the billowing smoke, Robin hollered back, 'There was no sign of anyone at the cottage. I left Marion safe and sound, making herself comfortable for the night.'

'Thank God for that.' Screwing his eyes against the orange heat, Tuck muttered an earnest prayer. 'At least one of us is safe.'

CHAPTER 15

The earl of Huntingdon threw his blankets back with an angry grunt. Only seconds before, he'd been clutching them so tightly to his neck, that his knuckles were white.

'Robert... No! My son, don't...'

The earl's cries echoed though the stiflingly hot bedchamber. As his nightmare curled his body into a protective ball, his arms reached out to grab hold of a figure that wasn't there.

Flailing in vain to catch hold of the spectre of his son, the earl's face contorted in pain and his hands slammed themselves again his ears. A hissing blast of livid spluttering flames filled his head. He could feel the heat on his face, his hands, and his legs as they kicked out blindly from within his dream.

'Get away from the fire! Run, Robert! Run!'

The reply that ricocheted through the earl's head was far louder than the fire that licked at his mind.

'YOU LIED!'

Tugging the blankets back to his neck, the earl whimpered like a child as his son's enraged, accusing, face pressed close to his.

'NO... no lies... You're my son, my heir... Run from the flames!'

Robert of Huntingdon, his clothing aflame, stood in the centre of the burning forest, his eyes full of hatred. 'There is another. You sired another...'

'No! Mathilda couldn't... your mother died... you know she did.'

Trying again to reach out to his heir, David of Huntingdon flinched with renewed pain as his son's words rebounded around his dream.

'Not from Mother. *From Margaret!* Margaret of Gisburne...'

'NO!'

The earl sat bolt upright, the action catapulting him awake as he sat in a tangle of sheets, his blankets half on and half off the bed. Sweat poured down his face as, disorientated, he tried to work out where he was. His thick grey hair was plastered to his head.

He patted the wooden bedhead behind him, needing to make sure it was real, and that the nightmare was over.

Reaching out shakily for the ale he kept by the bed, the earl's quivering hands lifted the cup to his mouth. He closed his eyes as the cool liquid slipped down his throat, but then opened them as the taste of ash and burning wood continued to coat his tongue, cloying it to the roof of his mouth.

Out of breath, as if he'd run all the way to Sherwood on foot, the earl saw the images of his dream fix themselves starkly to his minds-eye. 'Oh, Robert...'

Laying his head back on his pillow he muttered, 'Margret? Surely you would have told me if Guy was...?

'It's not true, Robert. It's a cruelty planted in your head by your mockers, son. It was a dream...' He scrubbed a hand over his forehead. It dripped with perspiration. 'It can't be true. Guy? My son?'

An image of Margaret's husband, Edmund of Gisburne, swam into his mind. His dark features creased, as they always had been, in scorn and anger. It was quickly followed by a vision of Guy's mocking face – his pale face, surrounded by blonde hair.

It can't be true.

Unsteadily, the earl swung his legs from the bed and yelled at the top of his voice towards the bedroom's oak door. 'Steward!'

Huntingdon's faithful aid was at his side in seconds, stifling a yawn. 'My Lord?'

'Help me dress.'

'But my Lord, you've only been abed a few hours, it's not long past midnight.'

'I didn't ask for the time! Get me dressed. I ride for Sherwood. Now!'

CHAPTER 16

The soldiers riding along the Newark Road watched the forest to either side of them with hawk-like vigilance. Each man wished he were back in his cot, rather than journeying through one of the most dangerous parts of Sherwood before sunrise.

In the midst of the soldiers, sat with confident arrogance, Robert de Rainault, Sheriff of Nottingham, kept his eyes fixed firmly forward He was too busy grumbling to pay attention to any danger that might be lurking in the trees around him; anyway, that's what he paid his guards for.

'Where's that oaf Gisburne when I need him? Trundles off to Normandy to try and make himself a hero. Typical! As if I've got time to crawl out of bed at the crack of dawn every time some baron or other gets into a temper. It's Gisburne's job to sort out these petty disputes and...'

The soldiers before him slowed, and the sheriff was pulled out of his latest stream of complaints concerning his absent deputy, as the horse in front of him came to a halt.

'Why have we stopped, Captain? I thought I made it plain that I was in a hurry to get this tiresome business over with.'

'I thought I could smell burning, my Lord Sheriff.'

'Oh did you?' De Rainault snorted as he rounded on the captain of the guard. 'You didn't just fancy a little rest, Jonas? Just because you've taken on some of Gisburne's duties doesn't mean you have to be as lazy as he is.'

'My Lord, I assure you.' The captain looked away from his master. 'I'm sure I can smell...' He stood up in his stirrups, craning to see through and above the trees. 'My Lord, I can see smoke!'

'Dear God, now what?' the sheriff groaned. 'You'd better check what's happening I suppose. Take three men with you, Captain. It's probably some clumsy forester whose let his bonfire get out of control. If it is, fine him. Heavily. The coffers are a bit low at the moment.'

'Yes, my Lord.' Jonas acted on the instant, determined to show the sheriff once and for all that he was worth three of that useless deputy, Sir Guy of Gisburne. 'You, you, and you. With me now. The rest of you, protect the sheriff with your lives!'

As he watched his captain ride into the forest, noting that he hadn't once muttered about the dangers of riding into Sherwood without checking for outlaws first, the sheriff smiled as he muttered, 'Protect the sheriff... umm... You'd better look to yourself when you get back, Gisburne. I can't remember the last time you protected anything but your own hide.'

A few minutes later the captain was back, his horse galloping at full pelt through the trees. His face was spotted with ash, and he spoke with a controlled panic that sent every hair on the back of de Rainault's neck standing up.

'Sherwood is on fire. A large circle of ash trees. It's bad, my Lord. The smoke's thick, but I could make out some men already tackling the other side of the blaze. We must dig around the flames to stop it taking the whole forest.'

Years of ruling over the shire immediately kicked in as the sheriff directed orders to the remaining men at arms. 'Two of you ride to the nearest village. Command every able-bodied person to help! The rest of you follow the captain. Use your cloaks to beat out the flames. And move fast!'

Jonas swung his mount round anxiously as the sound of his men's horses speeding towards their tasks quickly faded, leaving him and his master alone. 'But what about you, my Lord?'

He spoke calmly, but the sheriff knew his chief guard had, for the first time, registered that they were now alone in the middle of Robin Hood's lair, and what that could mean.

'Go and help your men!' The sheriff's head twisted towards the forest as the bellow of the flames increased. 'I'll ride back to Nottingham to get more help. I can take care of myself. Besides,' de Rainault looked anxiously into the woods, 'the king will have my head on a spike if he loses his forest.'

As he watched Jonas disappear between the trees, the sheriff circled his horse back towards the castle. A grim expression set on his face, 'Men already attacking the blaze... I wonder...'

***

The vicious inky liquid spat with renewed spite above the cauldron. Every now and then a black droplet would fly free from the clay bowl and hit one of the witches.

They didn't even flinch.

A single bead of ink splashed Marion's hand as it escaped the confines of the pot, surging with joy at the destruction of her home. Its sheer heat made her yelp in pain, but no one noticed. Within seconds, a blister was forming across the burn.

Cowering in the corner, forgotten for now, she struggled to breathe against the heat. Marion could see the door – the only way out of the cottage. But it was on the far side of the dwelling, beyond the witches.

There has to be away to get to it. There has to be.

Deep in thought, Marion jumped as a firm knock met the opposite side of the door on which she'd been concentrating. For a split-second, hope filled her. Could her friends have found her? Was it Oswald wondering who was in the cottage? One look at Morgwyn however, and her hopes turned to dust.

The sorceress gave a measured smile, her pitiless eyes fixing themselves on Marion as she bid the caller to enter. 'There's no need to knock outlaw, you can come in.'

Steeling herself to see a bewitched Robert of Huntingdon walk back in, a whimper shot from Marion's clenched lips as the door creaked open and the newcomer stepped inside. It wasn't Robert.

Her head shook from side to side.

It isn't him.

She hadn't expected to see him herself. To be this close. One or two steps forward and she could touch him… feel his hair, hold his hand…

He is dead.

Pressing her burnt hand against her chest, feeling as if all the air had been stolen from her, Marion gasped out a hoarse whisper. 'Robin of Loxley.'

The two witches laughed in derision at their distressed captive.

'Welcome back. You played your part well.' Turning from Loxley, Morgwyn addressed her sister. 'Rhawn, pass me the quill. It's a shame to end the charade, but we need our third witch to bring that charlatan of the forest to an end. Once and for all.'

Marion didn't want to look at Loxley, and yet she couldn't help herself because there he was.

Robin of Loxley.

Her husband.

He looked up at her through his dark brown fringe, just as he always had, as if nothing on earth was more precious than she was.

Here was the man who'd rescued her time and time again. The man who'd saved her from a boring life as the abbot's ward, giving her aimless existence a true purpose.

He is dead.

Licking her lips to try and force some moisture into them, Marion could taste the ink in the air as Rhawn rolled up the sleeve of Loxley's tunic. She wanted to reach out, to touch him.

To have him wrap his arms around her and tell her, just once more, that he loved her. She could hear him so clearly; her memory taking her back to the first time they'd met.

You are like a May morning…

As the words and visions of her past echoed through Marion's head, an image of Robert of Huntingdon arrived in her mind. He was smiling at her. They were dancing in a castle, there were candles and...

'Illam revertetur!'

Marion's confused reminiscences fractured back into the nightmare of reality as Morgwyn, the quill high once more, called out for a second time. *'Illam revertetur!'*

Watching in fascinated horror, too scared to move, Marion held her breath as Morgwyn placed the quill on Loxley's arm and began to write.

'Return her!'

No longer sure what was real and what wasn't, Marion hid her eyes from the image of the man she'd grieved over for so long and pressed her back against the wall of the cottage. But her respite from visions of the past didn't last long.

Enjoying the woman of Sherwood's distress, Rhawn took her prisoner by the wrist, yanking her forward. 'You will watch! See how the words seep into the flesh as the quill writes its enchantments and the image of your husband fades to the nothing he's become.'

Shaking within Rhawn's hold, Marion could only stare in disbelief as the figure of Robin of Loxley, so powerful in her own memory, faded away, transforming into the woman she'd been trying to save all along. *'Abertha?'*

Fury surged inside Marion as she spun around and lashed out at Rhawn with her free hand, scratching at the witch's face with her nails. 'What have you done to her?'

Ignoring her sister's cry of indignation at Marion's assault, Morgwyn snarled, 'Freed her of course! Unlocked her from false belief and saved her from living a lie! The enchantment of Lucifer runs in her blood now.'

'Freed her?' Marion's words rang with disgust as she studied Abertha. The sight was unsettling. Her husband's eyes and the novice's eyes still hadn't realigned themselves into their true form. 'How can making her look like the dead, free her?'

When Morgwyn didn't reply, Marion snapped. 'Abertha was Elana as well I suppose?'

'A roll she played to perfection.'

Addressing the girl, trying to ignore Rhawn's talon-like fingernails as the dug into her left wrist, Marion asked, 'Abertha, are you alright?'

'Perfectly, thank you.' The former novice smiled, and Marion found herself recoiling in shock.

'Don't smile like that! Don't you dare! That was his smile; that was the way he looked when I saw him in...' Pain and anger welled up within Marion as she whirled round, her free arm lunging across the limited space, sending a wooden table covered in bottles and piles of herbs crashing to the ground.

'You put the prophecy I saw in Herne's mouth. You enjoyed making him utter his lost son's name, knowing it would weaken him. Knowing it would hurt me!'

Striking the fallen table with her foot, Marion sent a clay pot skittering across the floor.

'Clear up the mess the woman's made Abertha.' With a contemptuous grunt, Morgwyn surveyed the debris around her. 'Rhawn, if you can't control her, I'll change my mind about letting you keep Huntingdon after we've finished with him.'

Marion's head shot back up. 'What did you do to Robert?'

'What do you think?' The sorceress drummed the quill against the side of the ink bowl.

Swallowing, Marion's eyes fell on the quill. She shuddered. It was just a thing to write with, yet she could have sworn she could feel the evil it exuded. 'You wrote on him, too...with that?'

'Such a simple idea, and so very effective.' Morgwyn held her weapon up to the light of the candles that lit the far side of the cottage. 'Herne's new son is so riddled with confliction that surprisingly little ink was needed to tame him.'

Marion mumbled, 'But Robert was himself, and then he wasn't quite right, but...' She broke off, lifting her chin proudly as she thought of all the times Robin Hood had fought evil and won. 'He won't ever be your puppet, even if you think he is!'

'The enchantment only works when I need it to.' Morgwyn shook her head in pity at her hostage's naivety. 'It's most amusing to see him switch from your Robin to mine. He doesn't even know he's doing it. The confusion on his hound's faces when he's with them is wondrous to behold.'

'You're mad!' Yanking as hard as she could, Marion freed her grip from Rhawn and sank to the floor. She didn't want to see the ink gurgling in the cauldron for another second, and she knew she couldn't get to the door without one of them stopping her.

I'll rest. Save my energy for when I need it. That's what Robin would do. What both Robins would do.

Rhawn bent to snatch the woman of Sherwood up again, but Morgwyn brushed her hand aside. 'Leave her to scrabble in the dirt, sister. Her home is on fire, she has nowhere else to go.' She glared down her nose at Marion. 'If you flounce around on the floor like that, you'll miss the show. Don't you want to watch your Robin Hood in action?'

'That's not *my* Robin Hood. That's *your* creature. Robert will fight. He's in there trying to get out, and I promise you he'll find a way. He *always* finds a way.'

'Not this time.' Morgwyn of Ravenscar spat upon the ground. 'Herne is weak. Helpless as Sherwood burns. Once the final point of the triangle is destroyed, Huntingdon will be the last Hooded Man to ever walk this earth.'

Sitting up abruptly, Marion rested her back against the solid cottage wall. 'What triangle?'

'The Hooded Man's strength – his power – comes from three sources.' Morgwyn's eyes blazed as she spun away from Marion and spoke into the ink. 'Herne, his master. Sherwood, his home. That just leaves his reason for being. His woman.

'That just leaves you to destroy, Marion of Leaford.'

CHAPTER 17

The noise was deafening yet, somehow, it also hung with an eerie tranquillity, blanketing out every other sound in the forest but for the shouts of the men who'd arrived on the opposite side of the blaze.

As the outlaws' drew back, abandoning their part in the battle against the flames, Will wiped his hand over his face. 'First time I've ever been glad to see soldiers.'

Coughing, trying to get the taste of scorched wood from his throat, John agreed. 'Feels wrong not helping to put the fire out.'

Robin rested his back against a tree, getting his breath back before he spoke. 'We can't risk it, John. You know the sheriff would sooner let the forest burn than miss a chance to capture one of us.'

With a final look at the flaming trees, the upper branches little more than naked twigs now, the outlaw's walked deeper into Sherwood with heavy hearts.

They'd only gone a few hundred yards when Much stopped, turning to look back the way they'd come. He could see smoke spiralling into the clouds. 'It is a real fire... isn't it?'

Will put an arm around his friend's shoulder, 'Smoke stinks real enough. And those aren't pretend bits of bark in your hair, Much.'

'I know but, well, strange things are happening. She could make us think there was a fire when there wasn't. Just like she made us see...' Spotting John and Will both madly shaking their heads behind Robin, Much stopped talking, but it was too late.

'Made you see what?

John ran a hand through his hair, causing a shower of crisped leaves to fall to the ground. 'While you were gone, well...' He cleared his throat. 'You remember what Marion said she saw in Herne's prophecy?'

'Ah.' Robin wiped his hands over his grubby face. 'Are you telling me that Robin of Loxley was here?'

Tuck nodded. 'Sorry, Robin.'

'You have nothing to be sorry for Tuck. This is her doing.'

Will grunted. 'Are we sure it's Morgwyn now, Robin?'

'I haven't had the chance to tell you. I went to see Herne. He told me it was her. She'd already ransacked his cave. Herne wasn't there - although he was. I can't really explain how.' Robin gestured towards a copse ahead. 'Let's rest here.'

Scarlet scratched his head as he sat next to Robin. 'But how did Morgwyn know about Elana?'

'You said that, when you met the Lady of the Cauldron before, she controlled your minds. What if she can get inside our heads and read our thoughts? What if she can see the experiences we've had in the past?'

Friar Tuck frowned. 'You mean she showed us Elana and Loxley precisely because they were people we loved and couldn't save. She'd have enjoyed that.'

Will grimaced. 'Yeah, well... maybe. That does make sense.'

'Gulnar could do that too though.' John scratched his blunt fingernails though her hair, as if to scour away his memories. 'He showed me dreams of not being able to save Meg.'

An uneasy scuffling of feet and murmurs of agreement caused Robin to bite down the temper he was surprised to find tightening his chest.

'It isn't him. Herne referred to Lucifer's Lady. And think about your first reaction when you heard what Herne said to Marion about the Lady of the Cauldron and the evil one. Morgwyn of Ravenscar is using our own memories to confuse us. She wants revenge for Loxley stopping her bringing forth the Devil.

'And if she can see into our minds, she's bound to see Gulnar. It wasn't so long ago when he...' Tuck paused as he caught Nasir's eye. He could see the Saracen was wondering the same thing he was.

'Robin, how did you know that Morgwyn called herself the Lady of the Cauldron? We've never told you that's what she liked to call herself sometimes.'

Robin shrugged, 'Marion told me on the way to the cottage.' He paused to scratch at his arm, dropping his eyes from the outlaws combined gaze.

'And Marion's definitely safe?' Tuck spoke carefully, as if wary of enraging a docile bee.

'I'd never have left her if she weren't.' Robin scratched harder at his arm as he peered over his shoulder. The sound of the fire was getting fainter.

Moving across the copse, Much came to sit by Robin's side. 'You alright, Robin? Does your arm hurt?'

'I think I caught it in the fire. It's fine.'

Without hesitation, Tuck reached out and took Robin's arm, yanking up the sleeve as he did so. 'Let me look. Once we've made it to one of our other camps, I'll make up a paste to... Oh. There's no burn, Robin.' Tuck caught Nasir's eye a second time. 'There's no mark there at all.'

Hurriedly rolling his sleeve back down, Robin smiled. 'Like I say, I just caught it. I was lucky. We all were.'

'How do you think the soldiers will put the fire out, John?' Much stood up, craning his head in a vain hope of seeing what was going on.

'They were beginning to hack back trees to create a barrier to contain it near to where I was. It'll stop the spread, but what's been lost won't be growing back anytime soon.' John didn't bother to hide the single tear that ran down his cheek. 'It's heart breaking.'

'It is.' Robin closed his eyes and fought to clear the fog that was suddenly clouding his mind, making his head pound and his thoughts muddled. 'You said you saw Loxley. It could have been him, or whoever it was Morgwyn made to look like him, who set the blaze.' As he spoke, the itch in his arm worsened and Robin couldn't help but to scratch at it through his tunic sleeve.

'You sure that arms alright, Robin?'

'We have more to worry about than my arm, Tuck.' Jumping to his feet, Robin patted his friend on the back. 'We need to move to our winter camp and find water. And then we need to think. That fire was too close for comfort.'

Much watched nervously at the smoke-grey sky. 'Do you think she'll start another one, Robin?'

'I don't know, Much. But I do know the sheriff's men are nearby and, while we need them to finish putting the fire out, we don't need them finding us.'

Tuck was still worried. 'But Marion won't know where to find us.'

'She will. Because I'm going to tell her.' Robin checked his arrows were undamaged before picking up his bow. 'Go to Darkmere. We know the soldiers are too afraid of the place to follow us there. I'll check on Marion and then I'll join you.'

Scarlet moved to Robin's side. 'One of us should come with you. It ain't safe out there. I'll come.'

'Thanks, Will, but that's why I want you to all stick together. Better just one of us risks a trip to Ollerton with so many soldiers about, not to mention sorcery. Once I'm back we'll work out how to find the missing woman Herne told Marion to save. Be careful. Trust no one.'

As they watched their leader disappear into the forest for a second time, Tuck said, 'He's worried about something.'

'Of course he is Tuck!' Will rounded, 'Sherwood's on fire, the woman he loves is hiding in a hut, miles away, and there's a lunatic witch on the loose!

Johns' mouth dropped open. 'The woman he loves! Of course. *The* woman!'

Will frowned, 'What?'

'Herne said, "Save the woman."' Fear lit up John's eyes. 'What if he didn't mean the nun?'

Tuck cried out. 'Little Flower!'

As one, the outlaws picked up their weapons and, without discussion, made ready to act.

Nasir pointed to the path Robin had taken. 'I will follow him.'

'I've got a really bad feeling about this.' Will scowled as Tuck rested a hand on his shoulder.

'You might be right to, Will.' The friar paused, uncertain if he should share his fear. A dip of encouragement from Nasir made him speak. 'What if Marion didn't tell Robin that Morgwyn called herself the Lady of the Cauldron?'

Scarlet interrupted, 'Tuck, you don't think that Robin is involved in this, do you?'

'I don't know, Will. But I do know he didn't burn that arm. He was rubbing at it when he was at the camp with Marion. Long before there was a fire.'

Swinging his staff around in the direction of Ollerton, John shuddered. 'We'll all follow him. Come on!'

CHAPTER 18

Crouching low, the outlaws watched the sheriff's men and local villagers working together to fight the fire. Each looked exhausted but determined as they faced the flames, a foe every bit as dangerous as the outlaw they dreaded encountering. The soldier's horses skittered restlessly on the far side of the clearing, a scorched space which was now five times larger than it had been the day before.

Will surveyed the scene. 'There's more soldiers than I thought.'

'Aye lad.' John kept low to the ground as he watched. 'Looks like they're stopping the flames spreading by pulling down the ground cover as well as digging a ditch. I reckon they're doing more damage than the fire!'

Tuck was thoughtful. 'I don't think she'll be very happy about the soldiers getting in her way.'

'You really think Morgwyn is behind this too, Tuck?' Will rose up on his elbows so he could get a better look at the sheriff's men digging fire breaks around the forest.

'Hell of a coincidence if not.'

Will chuckled. 'Hell of a coincidence... that's funny.'

Nasir raised his eyebrows just as he saw a familiar figure through the trees. 'Shh... The sheriff. He is here.'

'So he is. Watching but not helping.' Little John was surprised to see de Rainault risking his own safety near a burning wood. 'Let's slip past while they're still brushing soot from their eyes.'

Creeping forward, the outlaws stepped carefully. The previously clear pathway was strewn with fallen wood and smouldering leaves. Although the blistering groans of the fire would drown out most of the sound of their movement, they didn't want to make any noise if they could help it.

Ducking under a loose hanging branch, Much softly called over his shoulder, 'Go careful Tuck, there's a... Wait... watch out!'

The crash as the flaming branch fell from above, sent Much diving forward. 'Tuck!'

A second later, the friar emerged from a pile of twig dust. 'Don't worry, it missed me. Come on...'

The imperialistic tones of the captain of the guard rebounded across the enlarged clearing. 'Someone shouted *Tuck*. Didn't think Hood would be far away, my Lord.'

De Rainault, who'd been expecting an arrow in his back every minute since his arrival in Sherwood, yelled, 'Go on! If we can catch an outlaw the king might just be angry rather than livid when he hears about this.'

Jonas was already forming his men into an effective pattern for pursuit, which gave the sheriff another moment's thought as to the future of Gisburne, should he return from France with all his limbs intact.

'After them!'

Nasir drew his swords, twisting to face the others as he ran. 'They heard us, they're coming!'

Much muttered. 'I'm sorry, I...' as the twang of the first crossbow being fired across the forest echoed in their ears.

John pulled his arrow back to take aim. 'No time, Much, aim your bow!'

As the first volley of arrows left the outlaw's bows, Will shouted to Tuck, 'Crossbow to the left!'

A dagger cut through the air, and the soldier who'd been aiming at Tuck hit the ground with a thud muffled by the sound of running feet and the greedy rustle of the flames.

Nasir retrieved his knife. 'He won't be shooting at us again.'

John ducked low as he pushed Tuck ahead of him. 'Keep to the trees!'

They paused, firing another round of arrows into the forest. Two men fell as Will assessed their pursuers. 'There's only six, we can take them from here. Go after Robin, Nasir.'

The Saracen paused, 'One moment.' Another arrow hit its target. 'Five soldiers left. Now I go.'

Will grinned as he pulled back his bow again, calling, 'Be careful,' to Nasir as his arrow flew true, and another soldier hit the ground, his body smothering a patch of glowing embers. 'Four left. I make that one each.'

CHAPTER 19

The earl of Huntingdon was beginning to wish he'd listened to his steward and ridden with at least one guard, for company as well as protection. The crossroads, that would take him along the Newark Road, lay before him. He shuddered.

He'd been so sure that this was where he was supposed to be, but now he'd arrived he didn't know which way to go. Should he go on into the forest, or to travel onwards towards Nottingham?

Reining his horse in, he stopped and listened. Everything was still. He couldn't even hear a bird sing, and yet there was something... just on the edge of his hearing. The earl inhaled the scent on the wind.

'Smoke! The dream was right, there *has* been a fire.' He whirled his horse around, but then hesitated. He had no idea where to begin the search for his son. 'Where are you, Robert?'

A firm thump to his left made the earl's horse skitter as Robin Hood dropped from a tree onto the road. 'You called, Father?'

Patting his horse's mane to calm it, the earl smiled. 'I do wish you wouldn't jump out of trees like that!'

'You shouldn't have let mother teach me how to climb them, then.'

Laughing, his joy at seeing Robert alive easing the tension from his shoulders, the earl dismounted and slapped his son companionably on the back. 'If you think I had any control over your mother, you are very much mistaken. I'm relieved to see you, Robert.'

'You are?'

'Yes, I...' The earl paused as the sense of fear he'd tried to ignore on the journey elbowed its way back into his head. 'Are you alright, Robert? You were smiling a second ago, now you seem... troubled.'

Tethering the earl's horse, father and son walked in silence until they were the cover of the trees. When Robin finally spoke there was a resigned tone to his voice that made the earl wary.

'Troubled? That's hardly surprising is it? Sherwood's burning and I'm tired of people trying to kill me. Or lying to me.'

Hoping Robert didn't see him flinch, the earl rested his tired body against a tree. 'Lying to you?'

Robin leaned on the trunk next to his him. 'Why are you in Sherwood?'

'I'm on my way to see de Rainault.'

'Alone? I don't think so. That's another lie.'

'How dare you!' The earl's easy temper fractured. He'd ridden all that way, on his own, after a terrible night, just to make sure his son was fine, and then was accused of lying! And he *was* on his way to the sheriff. He fully intended to spend the night in Nottingham to recover before he rode home. 'I've never lied to you.'

'And yet you're doing it again right now!' Robin spun away from the earl, his eyes returning to the heart of Sherwood—the damaged heart. 'Why are you *really* here, Father?'

'Alright.' The earl held his hands up in defeat, 'But do you mind if we sit down. I'm not as young as I used to be, and it's a long ride from Huntingdon.'

As they sat beneath a broad oak tree, the earl looked into his son's eyes. Robin didn't even as blink. The earl shook off the new trickle of disquiet that made him swallow before he spoke. 'It sounds ridiculous, but I had a dream. It felt so real! You can imagine what my men would have thought if I'd told them I dreamt I had to find you, so I came alone.'

'You had to find me?' Suddenly, Robin's hostility faded to nothing, and he leant towards his father, anxious to hear more. 'What happened in the dream?'

Relieved to see his son's expression relax, the earl dismissed his son's unsettled demeanour as him being every bit as tired and fraught as he was himself. 'There was a fire. You were there. I thought...I thought I'd lost you.'

'I see.' Robin waved a hand behind him, 'There has been a fire, a big one, but as you can see, I'm alright.'

'And thank God for that!' The old man followed his son's eyes as they gazed into the depths of Sherwood. 'If I lost you, I could not bear it.'

'And that's why you came? Because you thought I was trapped by the fire?'

'Yes.'

Robin's brow creased. 'And the trip to Nottingham, are you really going there, or now that you've seen that I'm fine, will you return to Huntingdon?'

'I came because I was worried about my son. What's wrong with you Robert, why are you so brittle?'

Robin didn't answer. He stretched his legs out in front of him, flexing each one as he demanded, 'What else was in the dream father?'

A murder of crows began to caw overhead. A shudder went down the earl's spine as he continued to observe his son. 'I told you, I saw you in the fire. It was a dream Robert. A nightmare.'

Picking up a fallen twig by his side, Robin played it between his fingers. 'I'm sorry, Father. I just don't know what's happening at the moment. I feel as if I'm unable to control or stop whatever it is, and I'm worried. Someone is threatening the forest, me, and my men. Marion is safe for now, but...someone is putting ideas in our heads. Affecting our thoughts - maybe yours too. I feel like my mind is stuffed with fog. Nothing is clear. One minute I feel fine and then...Oh I don't know.'

As his son shrugged, the earl's face lit up in relief lit. 'But that must be it!'

'That must be what, Father?'

'In the dream I saw things that aren't possible. If you say someone is affecting people close to you, maybe it's affecting me too. That would make some sort of sense.'

'Maybe.' Robin patted his father's hand, a reassuring gesture in contradiction to his earlier accusations. 'Tell me more about the dream. It might be important. It could help me work out who might be doing this to us, to me.'

'Alright,' the earl paused, 'but it won't come as pleasant to you, Robert.'

Robin gave him a weak smile as he massaged his arm. 'I daresay I've survived worse. Tell me.'

'You've hurt your arm?'

'I caught it in the fire. Please Father, talk to me about the dream. Something tells me that time is running out.'

CHAPTER 20

Nasir moved through the forest with a rhythmic calm.

Despite his outward serenity he was worried. Following Robin Hood should be impossible. The outlaws had survived a long time in the forest because they made sure it was difficult to track any of them, but Robin's trail as he'd run from the camp was clumsy. It was as if...

He wants me to follow... or someone wants me to think *he does.*

Nasir stopped moving and listened. He could hear the dying sighs of the few trees which had been left to burn themselves out, the faint movement of the soldiers working in the forest, and the occasional caw of a crow, but nothing else. Yet, instinctively, he knew someone was close. He felt... watched.

He also felt confused. Robin had told them he was going to where he'd left Marion, but the evidence of his journey wasn't leading Nasir towards the hermit's cottage near Ollerton, but towards the Newark Road.

***

Wrestling with his growing impatience, Robin asked, 'Who else was in your dream apart from me, Father?'

'It was the sheriff's man. Gisburne. Guy...' The earl's voice petered off, unsure of how Robert would react if he went on.

'And?' Scratching harder at his arm, Robin could feel his agitation rising. The more he itched, the more impatient and frustrated he became by his father's lack of answers.

'Are you sure you're alright, Robert? If that arm's troubling you, you could come to Huntingdon. I'd see it treated and...'

'I'd be better if you'd just tell me! Don't you see! I must get back to Marion. Please, Father!'

The earl held up his hands in apology. 'Forgive me. I know it was nothing but a dream, but I'm wary of your reaction. I don't want to hurt you. I dreamt that...that you were not my heir. That it was...'

'Guy. '

The earl was startled. 'How did you—? Did they, whoever they are, show you the same dream too? It's nonsense of course. There's no way that...'

The quiet menace in Robin's voice made the earl shift away from his son's side. 'I've known for a while that you sired another.'

'What? But it was just a dream. You said...'

'It might have been a dream to you Father, but nonetheless it was the truth. All these years of lies...'

Panic gripped the earl's chest.

It wasn't true. It couldn't be. Could it?

He shook his head fervently, but the vision of Gisburne's blonde hair and Edmund's dark hair taunted him as Robert stood statue-still, glaring at him. 'It was just a nightmare; that's all. It isn't true!'

'Father, some time ago I spoke to Lady Gisburne. Was *she* wrong, too?' The abrupt quiet certainty to Robin's voice was more shocking than the words he spoke.

'Margaret? No, she'd have told me.'

'LIES!' Robin's shout echoed across the forest, and along the road.

'No! Robert, no.'

The earl as he scrambled to his feet. This was all wrong. Robin Hood would not make a noise in the forest. Whatever happened, the king of the outlaws would not leave himself vulnerable to attack like this.

Someone's got inside my son's head.

'Why can't you just tell me the truth?' Robert threw his arm back, ready to strike his father. 'The truth might hurt me, but at least I'd know where I stand!'

Stumbling backwards, the earl tripped on a tree root as he watched his son's fist bunch and his arm move in his direction. 'No, Robert! Please! Don't hit...'

The smack as Robin knocked the Earl of Huntingdon to the ground was dwarfed by the earl's cry of shocked pain. 'Robert!'

Robin stood over his father, his eyes expressionless. 'First, I'm mocked with Loxley, and now I'm mocked by you! Another betrayal.'

Wiping a hand over the blood pouring from above his eye where his son had punched him, the earl murmured, 'Son, I...'

'Be quiet!' The Hooded Man studied his victim's mystified expression for a second, before sprinting back into the forest.

With a groan, Huntingdon eased himself up onto his side, and stared at the place where his son had been. 'Robert... Come back, my boy...'

***

Nasir watched from the tree he'd positioned himself in, observing Robin's flight from the scene until the moment the forest swallowed him up. Then he jumped down and came to the earl's side.

'Lord Huntingdon. You're hurt.'

Wondering if he was dreaming again, the earl squinted up at the smiling Saracen. 'Nasir? My son, he...'

Helping the old man to sit up, Nasir spoke with his usual decisive economy. 'His mind is not his own.'

The seconds reassurance he'd experienced on seeing a friendly face, shattered as the earl asked, 'Did you hear what he said to me, Nasir?'

'I hear nothing.'

***

Abertha and Rhawn's fingernails dug into Marion's arms as she fought against their efforts to make her stand at the side of the cauldron. Clutching a handful of Marion's red hair, Rhawn used it as a lever to force her to look into the ink as it showed the world through the Hooded Man's eyes.

'The earl's an old man! How could you torment him like that?'

Morgwyn stood serenely on the opposite side of the cauldron. 'I didn't make him do that.'

'I don't believe you. Robert would never hurt his father.'

The sorceress shrugged, but kept her unfeeling eyes fixed on Marion. 'You can believe whatever you like – for now.'

Marion tried to shake her head, but Rhawn jerked her hair backwards. 'Your pretty man comes this way. I wonder if the welcome he has for you will be as warm as the one he gave his father?'

Unable to recoil from the stench of decay that emanated from the witch, Marion closed her eyes against the new vision, before issuing a private prayer to Herne. When she opened her eyelids again, she glared directly at Morgwyn.

'Is the earl alive?'

'I neither know nor care. I told you, the Hooded Man's words were not from my quill.'

'Liar! Gisburne is our sworn enemy! Robin's father would never...'

Morgwyn clapped sharply and Marion found her lips temporarily clamping themselves together while the sorceress shouted into her face. 'I said I don't care! You have an enemy much closer to home to worry about.'

Twisting on her heels. Morgwyn barked at Abertha, 'Come here, girl.'

Leaving Rhawn to hold Marion in place alone, Abertha joined her mistress on the other side of the cauldron. 'My lady?'

'The time is close. Roll up the woman of Sherwood's sleeve. I want the Hooded Man to show us how neat his handwriting is...'

CHAPTER 21

The sound of approaching hooves stilled Nasir's hand as he wiped the blood from the earl's face.

'I must leave you now, my Lord.'

Huntingdon gave his companion a grateful smile. 'You're a good man.'

The Saracen bowed as he stood up. 'As is your son. Do not forget who he really is.'

'I won't.'

The sound of a weaselly voice whining on the horizon blended with the pounding of approaching hooves. Nasir grinned. 'That will be the sheriff. Get to the side of the road. They will find you. I must go.'

'To find Robert?'

Nasir shook his head. 'To find who did this to him.'

***

'We've lost an acre! Over an acre maybe!'

Jonas was skilled at listening to his master, while, at the same time, paying very little attention to what he was saying. The sheriff, he knew from years of service in the ranks, enjoyed a good moan. As long as he agreed in the right places, all would be well. *That's where Gisburne went wrong. He tried to impress the sheriff by attempting to solve the sheriff's problems—and failing— rather than just listening to him whine.*

De Rainault gave an impatient tut as they turned right, following the Newark Road towards Nottingham. 'I can just imagine what King John will say when I tell him part of his forest has gone. He'll be ordering the noose to be tied around *my* neck before he's finished reading the message!'

The captain nodded sympathetically just as he caught sight of something moving in the trees out of the corner of his eye. 'My Lord... over there.'

De Rainault squinted to the roadside. 'What the blazes am I searching for, man?'

Jonas was already dismounting, passing his mount's reigns to the nearest solider. 'Just between the trees. Looks like a horse had thrown its rider, my Lord Sheriff.'

A soft groan travelled to de Rainault's ears. He was about to order the wretch to be left where he was, and declare that it served whoever it was right, and that they should be more careful when riding in the future, when Jonas called out again.

'My Lord Sheriff, it's the Earl of Huntingdon!'

'What?' Clambering off his horse, the sheriff hooked his cloak over his arm and ran to the fallen man's side.

'Sheriff?'

'My Lord, Huntingdon, what happened? Where are your men?'

The earl's hand came to his wounded head. His speech was slurred and sluggish. 'Alone. I came to find... The fire. My Lord, did you find any... Were there...?'

Understanding at once what the old soldier was asking, the captain replied quickly. 'We found no bodies in the fire, my Lord Huntingdon.'

'A mercy.'

The earl slumped back, relieved that none of Nasir's colleagues had come to harm.

De Rainault, assuming he'd been enquiring to his son's safety, refrained from comment as to whether that had really been a mercy. 'You're hurt, my Lord. What happened?'

Allowing Jonas to help him rise to his feet, the earl looked along the road. 'My horse reared and fled. I fell.'

The sheriff's eyes narrowed. 'Onto your face?'

'A minor cut. It's nothing.'

'No sign of your son? I thought he appeared, as if by magic, to aid those in trouble.'

Stung by the sheriff's words, despite how Robert had treated him that morning; the earl straightened his back and growled at the shorter man. 'You can never resist a dig at my family, can you, de Rainault? Even when a good word about you to King John might help in light of the damage to Sherwood, you still insult one of his earl's.'

Blustering, already cursing his rash words, the sheriff offered his arm for Huntingdon to lean against. 'Forgive me. Old habits. You'd be welcome at

Nottingham while you recover. Captain, find a horse for the earl. Do you think you could ride, my Lord?'

'I couldn't possibly impose. Perhaps, if I may have the loan of a horse and an escort to Huntingdon?'

The sheriff brushed again his objection, 'Nonsense. Gisburne is away. It would be good to have intelligent company for a change.'

'Guy is away?' The earl's blood raced as the reason for his disinclination to go to Nottingham was mentioned. 'Is he in London?'

'Normandy.' The sheriff scoffed. 'He's gone to play the hero. Assuming he didn't get lost on the way, and that he survived the sea crossing!'

Huntingdon was thoughtful, his eyes lost on the horizon. 'Fighting for his country, just like Edmund before him.'

'You knew Gisburne's father?'

'Not as well as I thought I did.'

De Rainault's forehead puckered into confusion. 'My Lord?'

'Forgive me, my head aches rather. I'm not quite myself.' The earl smiled at his host. 'Perhaps it would be wise to rest in Nottingham until tomorrow after all.'

CHAPTER 22

It had been a long time since Marion had either eaten or slept, but she knew that, somehow, she had to find the strength to fight on.

If I don't, I could end up like Abertha.

Repulsed by the thought of being one of Morgwyn's helpless minions, she tried again to picture Herne, to see him clearly in her minds-eye. But however hard she fought, his imagined image remained shrouded in a mist that she couldn't think through. Silently pleading with him to help her anyway, Marion kicked out anew, this time catching Rhawn on the knee, making her wince in pain and Morgwyn snort in derision.

'You're not going to take me over, too. You are *not*!' Marion's eyes were fixed on the quill that the sorceress held in her fingers, while Abertha attempted—unsuccessfully—to roll up her sleeve for a third time.

'Those hooded men like their woman strong.' Laughing without a trace of humour, the sorceress spun round and growled at her sister. 'Help Abertha. The quill is hungry. He'll be here soon.'

Panic leant Marion strength and she struck out again. Landing another blow on Rhawn's leg with the toe of her boot.

The witch jerked her body away from her, but without letting go of the tangle of hair she had wrapped around her fist. 'How dare you kick me!'

Shouting, 'Herne, protect me!' at the top of her voice, Marion lashed out again, wincing as Rhawn twisted, clawing at her hair even more.

Bored with the tiresome tussle that was going on before her, Morgwyn thrust a hand forward. Clamping Marion's face between her fingers, she dug her jagged nails into her prisoner's soft flesh, her words boiling on her tongue. 'Herne is *nothing*. He can't even protect himself!'

Morgwyn threw her captive to the floor as if she were worthless. Marion could feel Rhawn's hand immediately come back to her, wrapping her long hair around her fist, but she didn't react.

Surely her friends must be looking for her by now - except she'd seen in the ink that Robin had told them she was safe - so maybe they weren't on their way. Maybe it was all down to her now.

Only you can stop them.

Herne's voice echoed through her mind. But was it just her memory of the prophecy, or was his voice real now? Was he too summoning the will to keep up the battle against the power of the three witches?

Only you, Marion of Sherwood, Marion of Leaford. Only you can stop them.

Hope filled Marion. *He didn't say Marion Loxley!* It was Herne; somehow, he was there, sheltering in her mind.

Launching herself upwards, catching the witches off guard, Marion aimed her right boot at the table next to the cauldron, and kicked, hoping it would topple to form an extra barrier between her and the quill, buying her time for someone - anyone - to come and help her. She cursed as she missed her target, letting the coven's laughter at her failure add to her anger, and therefore her strength.

Marion panted for breath, pretending to weaken in Rhawn's grasp, before lashing out again, this time successfully hitting her gaol, sending the table next to the cauldron flying across the room.

Morgwyn shrieked as she held the quill close to her chest. 'Abertha! The cauldron! Protect the ink!'

Her magic is in the words she uses. That's what Robin said, and he was right! The ink! Of course, I must talk into the ink...

Marion saw her chance. Taking Rhawn by surprise, she darted towards the cauldron. 'Herne! Sherwood needs you.' She shouted over the rapid raging of the cauldron's fire. Her eyes widened and the ink, which had been dancing and spiking in tune with Morgwyn's mood, stilled for the briefest second, before it glugged back at her with pure hatred.

'You can't possibly think that'll work!'

There was neither time nor energy left to waste energy on replying to Morgwyn. Rhawn was desperately trying to grip both her wrists and pull hair at the same time. Marion wrenched one hand free and threw a punch at the middle witch's jaw.

Rhawn dived, dragging Marion with her as she dodged the blow. Tears of pain sparked in her Marion's eyes. Her hair felt as though it would be torn away at the roots, but still she fought against the hag's hold.

'For Satan's sake,' Rhawn cursed through gritted teeth, 'can't you bewitch her or something?'

Morgwyn shook out her long greying hair as she stood herself between Marion and the cauldron, uncaring that there was a fight going on around her. All that mattered was protecting the ink. 'We won't have to. Herne's Son will be here to do if for us soon.'

'No!' Marion scratched Rhawn's arm as tried to free herself.

'Well I wish he'd hurry up.' Breathless, Rhawn glared at Morgwyn. 'Why can't we just tie her up?'

'Because I'm enjoying watching your pathetic attempts at controlling her. And anyway, the more she rages at you, the weaker she becomes.'

Mustering her courage, Marion met Morgwyn's cruel eyes. 'Robin won't hurt me.'

'That is where we will have to agree to disagree.' Morgwyn tilted her head towards the door to the cottage as if she heard someone approach.

The second Morgwyn's attention moved from her to the door, Marion acted. Rather than pulling against Rhawn, she took her by surprise by slamming right into her side. As they collided, Marion pushed the witch backwards, so she fell, knocking the rim of the cauldron. The clay pot lodged over the hot fire slipped, slopping the liquid, so some lapped over its side and sizzled helplessly in the flames below.

Ignoring Morgwyn's cry of anger and Rhawn's moan of pain, Marion shouted into the remaining ink as it boiled and bubbled. 'Herne, help me. Help your son. Help the forest.'

As Rhawn refastened her hold on Marion, Morgwyn's face creased with scorn. 'Did you really think that would work against me?'

Muttering to herself over and over again, Marion chanted, projecting her voice towards the ink. 'He won't hurt me, He won't hurt me, He won't hurt me...'

Her heart skipped a beat as she saw Morgwyn, the quill held tightly, clap her palms over the pot. 'I told you, talking to the ink won't work for the likes of you.'

'And if I knock over the ink, will that work for me?'

'If you do that,' the sorceress hissed, 'then I'll stab each one of your arms and legs from here. I won't even have to move.'

Marion knew Morgwyn was telling the truth. She could have rendered her helpless over and over again without using anything as mundane as a rope, and yet she hadn't. *I wonder why?*

As the thought skittered through Marion's head, something clouded over Morgwyn's eyes. It was only a brief shadow, but when the witches' hand rose to her head, as if to soothe away a headache, Marion knew Herne was there. Somehow, he was continuing to battle against the powers of darkness.

Suddenly, the fog in her own head lifted, and Marion felt the Lord of the Trees speak to her.

Remember Tuck's teachings

Tuck's teachings? What did Tuck teach me?

Lunging towards the cauldron with renewed hope, Marion's foot just reached the leg of its stand, tilting it enough to rock on its platform before it settled again.

'Get her away from the cauldron!'

'I'm trying.' Rhawn growled as she propelled Marion back to the other side of the cottage. 'Why don't you do something to help me?'

'I need to save the magic for when he gets her.' The sorceress avoided her sister's eyes as she massaged her aching head. 'Abertha! Help Rhawn. You're supposed to be rolling up the woman's sleeve, not standing there like a gormless statute!'

'Yes, my Lady.' Snapping out her trance, Abertha made a dive for the outlaw's arm.

Summoning all her strength, Marion plunged forwards, burning her leg against the fire as she made the cauldron wobble with her foot; but still it did not fall. She thought furiously.

Tuck's teachings? Of course! Tuck taught me Latin.

Using the last of her might against the four hands that clawed at her, not pausing for breath, Marion spoke quickly into the spitting ink. '*Heme est celare familiae de medio ollae!*'

Rhawn looked frantically at the former abbess. 'How does she know what to say?'

Marion spun around and glared at her captor. 'It's just Latin you stupid woman. You helped enchant the ink, you should know that!' Then she threw a fresh punch which sent Rhawn sprawling across on the floor.

Morgwyn ignored the growing chaos around her, as Abertha hauled Marion back from the precious potion. Instead she collected up a small pot from where it had been knocked to the floor and, almost reverently, used it to scoop a tiny quantity of the ink from the cauldron. Once a fraction of her treasure was safe however, her temper broke.

'Enough of this! Rhawn, get up.'

As Rhawn crawled towards her sister, Marion felt an unseasonably cold gust of air flow through the stifling heat of the cottage. Goose-pimples dotted her skin as she dodged the slap of Abertha's hands as the novice tried to slap her.

'Please wake up! Please! Abertha, get off me. I'm here to help you!'

The third witch's hands fell abruptly to her sides and her determined expression became serene. At first Marion thought the novice had heard her pleas, but as the breeze whistling through the cottage became stronger, she realised she had nothing to do with Abertha's abrupt calm.

Where's the wind coming from?

The door hadn't blown open, nor was the one tiny window undone.

Marion risked a glance at Morgwyn. The former Abbess of Ravenscar's head was held high, her shoulders pulled resolutely back… but Marion could see uncertainty growing in her flint eyes as the breeze began to whisper.

'*The little flower belongs in the forest…*'

'NO!' The scream that left Morgwyn's lips shook the foundations of the cottage as her sister grabbed at her leg.

'Is that…?'

Morgwyn shook her head quickly, as if trying to dislodge a troublesome insect. 'No, it can't be… we banished him… he's gone now…' Her voice wavered as the breeze spoke again; present and yet, at the same time, faraway.

'*The Hooded Man shall come to the forest to be Herne's Son and do his bidding…*'

The mention of the Hooded Man spurred Morgwyn back into action. She'd worked too long and too hard for her revenge to have it snatched from her fingers now. 'Abertha, don't just stand there. Rhawn, I told you to get up!'

Herne's voice, growing more solid all the time, echoed around the hermit's cottage. '*Spill the ink!*'

Marion leapt back to her feet and rushed forward, only to be caught by Morgwyn, who threw her sideways into Rhawn's waiting arms.

'Abertha, get that sleeve rolled up. Do it now!'

Obeying at once, Abertha took Marion's arm as Rhawn, determined not to humiliate herself further, took a tight hold of their hostage.

'*Spill all the ink!*'

Marion cried out as she strained her muscles in an attempt to reach the cauldron.

'If you spill that ink then you'll kill the nun *and* your man.' Morgwyn crowed from the far side of the room, the small clay pot and quill tight against her body. 'The ink is in their blood. It's their life force. Soon it's going to be yours too.'

'Robin would sooner be dead than your puppet!' Hoping the same could be said for Abertha, Marion gave a final kick, and the ink filled bowl flew from the top of the cauldron, toppling to the ground with an ear-splitting crack.

Morgwyn's shrieks of rage were only equalled by Abertha's yelps of pain as she was splashed by the scolding ink, which coated the walls and floor.

Marion tried not to think about the burns forming on her own arms as the ink splattered the cottage. Instead she bunched up her strength and hit Rhawn square in the face, sending her flying backwards so fast that she hit her head against the stone wall, and lay unmoving. Not wasting time savouring the victory of having one less witch to worry about. Marion fell to Abertha's side. The novice was on her knees coughing hard, gulping for breath.

'So thirsty, I'm...' Her eyes had closed and she'd slumped to the ground before Marion had been able to utter a single word of comfort. 'Abertha?'

Morgwyn, her clothing smeared with black, her hair full of cloying ink, unmoved by her kin's unconscious state, scoffed, 'You've killed her, Marion of Sherwood. How long before your Robin Hood falls to the ground as well?'

'You did this, not me!' The reality of what she'd done hit Marion as she stared helplessly at Abertha's body.

'Why do Herne's outlaws never learn? You can't defeat the servants of Lucifer. Not ever.'

Morgwyn clicked her fingers, and the door to the cottage flew open. 'At last!'

Robert of Huntingdon strode into the room, his unblinking eyes surveying the wreckage, his expression devoid of emotion.

'No.' Marion sank to her knees. Herne had told her what to do and she'd done it. But still it wasn't enough.

Marion avoided looking at Morgwyn's triumphant expression as the witch grabbed her and bunched up the sleeve of her dress.

'Take hold of your woman Robin Hood. And keep her still! There is just enough ink left in this pot for the quill, and it's so very hungry.'

CHAPTER 23

Rufford Abbey's bell was tolling noon as Nasir reached the crossroads in the forest path which led to either the village of Ollerton or the orchard and hermit's cottage. Secreted between the trees, the Saracen sniffed as a gentle wind sent wafts of wood smoke to assail his nostrils and prod his taste buds, so different from the acrid stench of the fire raging on the other side of Sherwood. He frowned, there was another smell too, something he didn't recognise - something cloying, burnt and sour.

Scanning the stretch of ground that lay between him and, ultimately, the orchard that neighboured the cottage, Nasir knelt, so his eye-line was closer to the earth.

'Flattened grass, torn leaves... Robin is clumsy.' Muttering under his breath he sidled along the path that led to the cottage. Nasir paused again. 'Too many broken twigs.'

The crack of a leaf being crunched under a boot sent Nasir further into the shadow of the trees. His right hand had already drawn a dagger when he relaxed and stepped forward. 'You took your time.'

John grunted, 'The sheriff's captain is more efficient than Gisburne. There were extra soldiers on the far side of the fire.'

'Yeah.' Will looked worried, 'The smoke had hidden them. We're gonna have to keep an eye on that particular soldier in the future.'

'In the future yes,' Tuck snapped, 'but right now we're here, and we have more important things to do! Are we sure Robin is in the cottage?'

'He definitely passed this way.' The Saracen nodded. 'We need to get closer to be sure he's inside.'

Nocking an arrow to his bow, not sure if he wanted an answer to the question, Much asked, 'Was Tuck right about Robin?'

'I think so.' Nasir gestured towards the trampled grass ahead of them. 'Someone's taken his mind, but not all of it I think.'

Scarlett peered about them as he snorted, 'We ain't got time for guessing games 'ere Nasir. What do you mean?'

'He is divided. In two minds. One half laid a path for me to follow. It breaks off sometimes, but then it returns. The other half of his mind belongs to Morgwyn.'

'Right.' Will drew his sword. 'We should get closer.'

The outlaws had only travelled a hundred yards when a terrifying cry erupted from the distant cottage.

'Little Flower!'

Tuck was already running towards the orchard, his corpulent frame wobbling as he made a beeline for the hermitage on its far side. His friends quickly overtook as they ran towards Marion's pleas for help.

Keeping pace with Scarlet, Much lifted his bow ready to fire as they ran. 'What do we do when we get there?'

'Whatever we 'ave to.'

***

Marion looked into the eyes of the man she loved, but there was no sign of the kindness she was used to seeing there. The compassion and drive to help others that had bought him to Sherwood to be Herne's Son in the first place was shrouded in enchantment.

'Robin!' She struggled helplessly against his hands as he dragged her towards the light of the cauldron's fire, 'Please, please… Robin, wake up.'

The spilt ink and broken pots were forgotten now as Morgwyn, radiant with the taste of victory, stepped forward, the quill and pot of ink held out before her. 'Take the quill Hooded Man. Write the Woman of Sherwood's fate on her flesh.'

'Oh Robin…' Marion could still feel a light breeze on her face, but since the arrival of his son, Herne had become distant again, as if pushed back by the power of Morgwyn's determination to steal his protégé from him.

'My pleasure, my Lady.' Robin bowed as, holding both of Marion's wrists securely in one hand, he took the quill with the other and slowly lowered it into the ink.

'Don't you dare write on me!' Gritting her teeth, Marion willed herself to think. *I must knock over the pot of ink. Herne said it all had to be spilt.*

Robin loomed over her, holding the quill aloft as if he were about to wield

Albion and deliver the final blow against an enemy.

I must spill the ink. I must snap the quill.

As Robin crouched to her side, his grip weakened slightly on her wrists as he concentrated on lining up the quill. Marion seized her chance. Lunging forward, she broke free, and took hold of Robin's right hand with both of hers, wrenching the fragile quill from his fingers.

The animalistic screech that shot from Morgwyn's lips was deafening as Marion tore at the slim feather, bending it until it snapped and the poisonous tip hung at its side, its reservoir of ink dripping uselessly to the floor. With one more tug, Marion broke the nib completely free and threw it as hard as she could at Morgwyn.

In her desperation to catch the fragments of her weapon, Morgwyn fumbled, dropping the last remaining pot of ink, which skidded across the stone floor. It smashed to pieces in the corner of the room, leaking black ink over its fractured shards.

Breathless, Marion sank down, backing away from both Robin and Morgwyn as fast as she could.

The sorceresses rage rebounded around the hermitage. 'The quill... It's broken. Quick outlaw, your dagger. KILL HER!'

Robin's pulled his dagger from his belt, his eyes dulled as he took hold of Marion's left ankle and yanked her towards him. 'Time to join Loxley, Woman of Sherwood.'

'ROBIN! Wake up! The ink's gone. You can come back to me!' Frantic, Marion covered her eyes as she yelled at the top of her voice. 'Herne, where are you? Will, John... Anyone! Help me!'

Morgwyn's laughter cracked with hysteria as Robin's dagger moved towards its target. 'Herne is weak, Sherwood is damaged and the woman *shall* die.'

'No...'

Marion closed her eyes as Morgwyn bawled out the order. 'Kill her! Do it now!'

Smiling, Robin thrust the dagger forward as Morgwyn raised her hands, bellowing, 'Lucifer! Receive thy sacrifice!'

Rolling onto her side, her years of self-preservation telling her when to dodge the blow kicking in just seconds too late, Marion screamed as Robin's knife entered her flesh.

'At last!' Morgwyn raised her hands high above the fire in triumph. 'The triangle is broken. Lord Lucifer is revenged! Now nothing can prevent me freeing my master from the bounds of hell.'

CHAPTER 24

The silence after the final scream was worse than the cries the outlaws had heard as they ran towards the cottage.

'We're coming, Little Flower!' Tuck puffed as they finally arrived at the side of the cottage.

'What the hell is happening in there, John?' Will raised his dagger, ready to punch the door in.

'Don't ask me, lad.'

Much looked around the side of the cottage, checking that no one else was there. 'How will we get them out?'

'We haven't got time to plan. Let's just...' Will's hand was on the cottage door, but he dropped it again as Herne's voice boomed across the clearing.

The Hooded Man shall come to the forest, to do MY bidding.

Spinning around, trying to see where the voice of Herne had come from, Will staggered backwards as the cottage door crashed open and Robin stumbled outside. He held Marion, pinning her before him, his arm almost garrotting her neck.

'Robin?' Much looked at his fellow outlaws in dismay as their leader reeled forward.

Swaying, his face distorted in confusion, Robin let Marion fall to the ground, as he crashed down next to her clutching at his head.

Much went to dash forward, but Will caught his hand.

'Stay back, Much.' He whirled his sword out in front of him, keeping the blade between the outlaws and Robin.

'But he's hurt Will, and so is Marion. Come on!'

'I said no, Much!' Will glanced at John, who nodded grimly.

'We don't know who is in the cottage, lad.'

'But Marion, she's bleeding. We can't just stand here, John.' Tuck unhooked the bag he was carrying, ready to go to her side.

'Tuck, wait. Look at him...' John backed further away from the figure of Herne's Son. His eyes were open and his face was blank as he writhed on the earth, brawling with whatever had taken over his head. 'That isn't Robin. Not yet.'

'Well I don't care! It's my fault she's here! Marion needs me.'

John managed to haul Tuck back to his side just as Morgwyn, her clothes ruined, her face haggard, emerged from the cottage.

With a strength born of desperation, Morgwyn hauled Robin up to his feet by the neck, squeezing his throat as she dragged him towards her, holding him like a shield. 'The ink was spilt, so why aren't you dead?'

Only then did the witch notice the outlaws.

'So you did bother to turn up then.' She gave a manic giggle as her foot struck Marion's side. 'She'd quite given up on you rescuing her you know.'

Will pulled back his bowstring as the witch shouted into the canopy of trees above them. 'You're too late, spirit. He's mine!'

The air stirred faster, rustling the leaves above as Herne's voice bounced off the trees. *'Robin of Loxley was Herne's Son. Robert of Huntingdon is Herne's Son.'*

She bellowed at the sky, 'Show yourself you coward.'

Herne's calm voice enraged her further as he whispered, *'I am always here. I am the trees and the wind and the soil.'*

There was a crack as the breeze suddenly swirled up in a cloud of dust, forming into a targeted blast of air, which aimed itself directly at Morgwyn.

The outlaws watched, transfixed as the former Abbess of Ravenscar, her hair blowing around her shoulders, tried to move her feet. But she couldn't lift them. Letting go of Robin, she pulled at her legs, wrenching with all her might. 'What have you done? I can't move.'

'You are my prisoner.'

Tiny tree roots sprang from the ground, furling themselves over the sorceresses' filthy bare feet like writhing snakes, pinning her in place.

'You were banished! Sherwood is wounded and Marion is dying. The triangle *is* broken.'

'I am their guide. Sherwood is their home. Marion of Leaford is their heart. The power of three remains. So must it be...' The whirl of dust blew up from the ground, twirling faster around Morgwyn, blurring the outlaw's eyes as Herne's voice commanded, *'AWAKE!'*

The dust cloud subsided as quickly as it had arrived. The outlaws hadn't dare move before, but now they ran to Marion's side.

'Marion?' Tuck lifted her arm. 'There's a lot of blood. Much, open my bag. I need a large cloth for a bandage.'

As Marion's eyes fluttered open, Nasir took up a position between Morgwyn and his friends. He drew both his swords, crossing them before his chest, his eyes daring the sorceress to speak.

She didn't say a word but stood pulling at her feet with all her might, sending spell after useless spell at the roots that bound her in place.

'Tuck?' Marion blinked in the afternoon light. 'Robin, he... My arm... blood... Is he alright?'

The friar smiled as he wiped a cloth over her clammy forehead. 'He's alive.'

Herne's voice came again, softer this time. *'Hear me Marion of Sherwood, only you can end this.'*

Raising herself a fraction, wincing with pain, Marion shook, dizzy through loss of blood. 'But how?'

'You know how.'

Marion took her time to sit up. She ignored Tuck and Much's intake of breath when they saw the mass of tiny burn blisters caused by the spattered ink, and the scratches from Rhawn that adorned her hands and arms. Nor did she comment on the stab wound, which Tuck had tied beneath a linen strip.

'Yes, I think I do know.'

Shuffling on her knees, not wanting to put any weight on her arm, Marion sat beside the vacant figure of the earl's son. He seemed lost as she placed a finger under his chin and reached in to kiss him.

'I love you, Robert of Huntingdon... Robin Hood... Herne's Son. And I always will.'

Will caught John's eye. 'That ain't gonna work. This ain't no ballad.'

Robin lifted his head, his eyes clearing as he whispered, 'Marion?'

John dug Will in the ribs as they watched. 'Wrong again, lad.'

'Yeah,' Will whispered, 'but in the ballads the hero don't hate himself forever for what he's done, even when he couldn't help it.' Scarlet turned away from Robin's expression. It was so full of realisation and self-loathing that it was painful to behold.

Robin gingerly reached out a hand and ran it across Marin's dirty face. 'It is really you, isn't it?'

'Yes. It's me.' She stroked a blonde strand of hair and tucked it behind his ear.

Robin stared at her arm. He tried to form the words, but nothing felt right. 'I'm so sorry.' It didn't seem enough but it was all he had. 'What have I done to you?'

'I'm alright.' Marion smiled bravely but winced as Robin reached out to touch the arm that had so recently met with his dagger.

Registering for the first time that his friends were there too, Robin clambered to his knees. 'Tuck! Her arm... I... I stabbed it.'

The friar soothed Robin's head with a fresh cloth. 'You've had a fever. You need to rest.' He switched his gaze to Marion, 'you both do.'

'It's just my arm.' Giving Tuck a grateful smile, Marion added, 'Thank you for teaching me Latin back when we were both living in Nottingham castle.'

'Latin?' Tuck gave a puzzled smile. 'You hated learning it. What made you thank me for that now?'

'I'll tell you later.' She returned her attention to Robin.

He looked forlorn as he held out a hand towards her, not quite daring to touch. 'I almost... I was going to...'

'But you didn't. Tuck will care for me. I'll be fine.' Marion ran a hand through her hair. It was tangled and knotted from where Rhawn had held it tight for so long.

Nodding dumbly, Robin looked up at the other outlaws. 'I don't know what to say?'

'As long as you're back with us then you don't have to say anything.' John grinned. 'Arm stopped itching has it?'

'What? Oh, yes...There was this quill, it...' Robin's eyes landed on Morgwyn for the first time since he'd come back to himself. He rose unsteadily to his feet, his expression fixed and unwavering, his tone resolute. 'Let's finish her properly this time.'

'Keep away.' Morgwyn, unable to move her feet, waved her arms in front of her face in a frantic attempt to shield herself. 'Keep away!'

'Why, what are you going to do, turn my men into dogs that bark for you? Not this time!'

Robin swung around, Albion already in his hand as he called to Much: 'There are two more women in the cottage. See if they're alive.'

'Yes, Robin.'

As Much ran inside the former hermit's home, Robin signalled to Will, Nasir and John. 'Surround her! This time we have to make sure she's truly dead.'

Stepping closer, swords drawn, the outlaws closed in on their captive.

In a desperate attempt of bravado, Morgwyn shouted at Robin. 'You think you can scare me! Fools! Kill me, and I go straight to my master.'

'Who you've failed,' Robin stated. 'Twice. Are you so sure you'll have a warm welcome?'

Much backed out of the house. 'The nun, Abertha, is dead. There's another woman too. Unconscious.'

'Guard her well, Much. Her name is Rhawn. She is this creature's sister.'

Will hissed, 'Let me finish her Robin. She tortured me with memories of Elana. She showed us, Loxley. The hag deserves it.'

'You're right, Will. She does.' Robin lunged forward, Albion high in his hands as Morgwyn's shrieks were drowned out by a command from Herne.

'No, my son. Leave her to the forest.'

Robin, breathing hard, his face red with anger, immediately lowered Albion.

Scarlet on the other hand, was spitting mad. 'But she don't deserve to live.'

Will's frustration was lost in the wind as Herne's voice filled the clearing. *'Take the body of the girl to the monks. Robin is to take Marion home. You will not see Morgwyn of Ravenscar again.'*

CHAPTER 25

The evening light flittered thought the leaves above, reflecting on Robin and Marion as they sat alone by the bonfire. They had reached their traditional winter camp, hidden away in the part of Sherwood known as Darkmere, holding hands, but walking in silence. On arrival, they'd taken comfort in the familiar tasks of lighting the fire, finding water to drink, and rummaging through the scant food stocks to find something from last year's supplies to take the edge of their hunger.

Now however, as moonlight flickered across the clearing, they couldn't put off talking about what had happened any longer.

Robin pulled up his hood against the cool evening air, the act helping to hide his shame.

'I was me, but I wasn't me. She wrote on my arm and then...The fire in Sherwood. It was me. I started it. I wanted to. The desire to see the forest burn was overwhelming.'

Laying a hand on his, Marion watched the lick of the campfire. The flames were so much friendlier than the oddly vertical blaze in the hermit's cottage. 'It wasn't you, it was her.'

'But it was still me that threw the torch into Sherwood.' Robin paused, swigging back some water before he went on. 'And then... I met my father.'

'I know.' Marion rested her head on his shoulder, relaxing her stiff arm as best she could. 'She made me watch in that cauldron of hers.'

With a strangled groan, Robin picked up a stone and played it between his fingers. 'Then you heard what I said and saw that I attacked him. I could have...' His words faltered as he threw the stone into the trees. 'I could have killed him.'

Feeling Robin's pain, Marion squeezed his palm in hers. 'Go to the earl tomorrow. Explain that it was all lies, that Morgwyn planted in your head. He'll forgive you.'

'Lies... umm.' Robin flipped his hood back and looked at Marion. Her face was clean now, but it would be a while before the bruises heeled, not to mention the wound in her arm, which he doubted would never be as strong again. 'And you? Will you forgive me?

'There is nothing to forgive. She told you to kill me, but you didn't.' Leaning forward to kiss his nose, Marion of Sherwood smiled. 'Herne gave you the powers of light and darkness. Morgwyn let out the darkness, but the lightness won.'

'But...' Robin got to his feet and began to pace, his head still thudding with the aftereffects of the ink. 'I knew what I was doing, but also, I didn't. Could I have fought harder? What if there was some part of me that wanted all that to happen?'

'Of course there wasn't.' Marion stayed where she was, letting him walk off his anger.

'But, don't you see, Marion? I'm not sure I know who I am anymore.'

Alarm grew inside her, but Marion kept her voice calm as she said. 'Well I know. I've always known. You are Robin Hood, you are Robert of Huntingdon, you are Herne's Son – and I love you.'

'Do you?' Robin shook his head sadly. 'All three of me? Or just one part?'

***

There were still broken pieces of pottery on the floor, but the cavern no longer looked as if a storm had ravaged it.

Herne was there, his presence fully restored, his headdress laid across the altar to his side. He was stirring at a large metal pot. 'You are troubled.'

'I could have killed Marion.'

'Herne's Son could never kill his woman.'

Robin gnawed at the inside of his lips, the hope he'd tried to build as he'd fled from Marion to Herne's cave dying like the last embers that glowed in the forest. 'Morgwyn was right then. Marion only loves me because I'm your son. Not because I'm me. When the others saw Loxley, I...'

Herne threw a handful of herbs into his potion and closed his eyes. 'He *was* my son. You *are* my son.'

Robin's tone was strained as he asked, 'And there will be another?'

The Lord of the Trees tilted his head up, holding his son's gaze. 'Morgwyn's magic lay in doubt. I tried to counteract it by planting a fog of my own within your head, but her magic was strong.'

'You shrouded me in the fog? You gave me the headache.'

'To protect you.'

Massaging his forehead, Robin nodded. 'So, I left a trail for Nasir to follow, because of you?'

'Because I gave you a tiny space in your head where you could think for yourself. Yet, it wasn't enough. Morgwyn still managed to release your worst fears and insecurities. Don't let her win by allowing those doubts to consume you.'

Exhaling, Robin asked, 'What did you do with her?'

'She resides where only the Hooded Man, the forest, and the woman can call her back, but they will not do so.'

'Sherwood consumed her?'

'There will be a new tree in the forest tonight.'

Robin shuddered, wondering if some of the darkness Marion had spoken of had leaked into Herne's soul. 'And her sister?

'Has no memory of what's happened.' Herne beckoned to his son, his attention remaining on the bowl before him, as if he were watching something. 'She heads to Wales.'

Not wanting to see either Morgwyn or her sister ever again, Robin stayed where he was. 'I'm not sure I can be your son anymore.'

Herne picked up the silver arrow that lay on the stone table next to him. He weighed it in his hands. '*You*, Robert of Huntingdon, *are* Herne's Son. I called and you answered.'

Robin pulled Albion from his side, his eyes running along the runes that decorated the blade. They glittered in the candlelight as he heard Herne repeat the words he'd vowed to follow.

'Bring hope to those who have none, freedom to those in chains, justice to those who have been wronged.'

'But I hurt Marion. I hurt Sherwood.'

'They will mend stronger than before.' Moving to his son's side, Herne pushed Albion back into Robin's belt. 'Sherwood, Marion and I remain. The power of three is strong. The triangle is unbroken.'

Robin reached out and stroked the silver arrow. 'But how long will it be before someone tries to break again?'

It was almost midnight when Will, Tuck, Nasir, John and Much returned from Rufford Abbey. Their faces were flushed in such a way that told Marion they'd stopped off in Ollerton to sample some more of Oswald's mead. She sighed. They'd been giving Robin and her time to be alone. An unnecessary kindness.

It was Scarlet who first noticed that only one figure sat by the fire. 'Marion?'

The intoxicating effects of the mead faded as John knelt beside her. 'Where is he, lass?'

Marion was still forming the words to try and explain when she found herself engulfed in the comfort of Friar Tuck's arms as he sat beside her, his expression bleak.

'I don't know. But he'll come back.' She gave her friend's a weak smile. '*He will*. I can feel it.'

CHAPTER 26

Robin had been watching for the horse since dawn.

This time his father wasn't alone, but he'd expected that. De Rainault valued the earl of Huntingdon's position in the eyes of the local barons too highly to let him travel all the way home alone; even though he despised the man's son.

Waiting until the party of three was only a few yards away, Robin lowered himself from the tree and strode into the middle of the road, hoping his father would acknowledge him, before the guards took it upon themselves to shoot.

With a bark of orders to the guards to rest by the side of the road, and, if they knew what was good for them, not to mention to the sheriff that they'd seen Robin Hood that day, the earl hailed his son.

'Robert.'

Not wasting time, Robin reached out a hand to help his father dismount. 'I've been trying to think what to say. I'm sorry. You're badly bruised.'

'Falling from a horse can do that at my age.'

Robin frowned, 'Falling from a horse? But you didn't fall, I...'

With a firm shake of his head, the earl repeated, 'I fell from my horse.'

'I don't deserve that.'

'Shall we sit down?' The earl walked to the side of the road, gesturing for Robin to join him. 'We've all done things we regret. Why should you be different?'

Shifting awkwardly, Robin confessed, 'You weren't the only one I hurt.'

The earl watched his son for a moment, before laying a hand on his shoulder. 'Nasir said you were not yourself. That the person you told me was messing with your thoughts was using sorcery.'

'You saw Nasir?' Robin raked a hand through his hair.

'He came to my aid after... after the last time we met.'

A new hit of shame engulfed Robin as he muttered, 'Nasir is a good man.'

'So, he hasn't said anything to you about what we talked about?

Robin's head jerked up, 'You think he overheard our conversation?'

Tilting his head to one side, the earl took in his son's puffy, sleep deprived eyes and dirty clothes. 'You didn't know I'd seen Nasir because you haven't been back to talk to your men yet, have you?'

'Not properly, no.' Robert found he couldn't meet his father's eyes as he asked, 'How much do you think Nasir heard?'

'Everything; but he swore he hadn't heard a word.'

'Then he'll say nothing. Nor will Marion.'

Huntingdon groaned, 'She knows too?'

'Morgwyn, the sorceress responsible for all this, she was observing us somehow, and made Marion watch too. Marion is convinced what we, umm... discussed... is a lie of Morgwyn's invention. I didn't argue with her, but I didn't like lying.'

'Because you are a good man.' The earl laid a hand on his son's arm. 'Herne chose wisely.'

Robin swallowed again his dry throat. 'Father...'

Guessing what he was about to say, the earl held up his hand. 'No, Robert. No good will come of it. If what I saw in my nightmare is true, then I swear on my love for your mother, I did not know of it. Outlaw or not, when my time comes, you'll have to choose. King of Sherwood or Earl of Huntingdon. Whatever your answer, no other will be offered the earldom on hereditary grounds.'

Silence rested over them for a while, each man lost in reminisces, both pleasant and painful, before Robin spoke again.

'May I ask a favour I don't deserve?'

'You may.'

Robin licked his lips, his eyes fixed on the horizon. 'Can I come back to Huntingdon -for a while at least? If I leave Sherwood, Herne will find another son who deserves Marion more than I do. Herne's Son will always love Marion of Leaford. It doesn't have to be me.'

Stunned, as his son requested the last thing he'd been expecting, David of Huntingdon asked, 'How did the witch make you hurt her?'

'A knife in her arm. It was supposed to be her heart, but...'

'But, even under the influence of sorcery, you couldn't kill her.'

'Herne said I could never kill her because I was his son,' Robin shrugged, 'that's how I know another will care for her. Another who won't be able to kill her because he'll love her too much, simply because he will be Herne's Son as I am now, as Loxley was before me.'

'My poor boy.' The earl could see Robert's pain and remorse reflect in his eyes and knew his son's guilt went beyond the knowledge of the physical injury he'd inflicted on Marion. 'Tell me, has she have forgiven you? And Scarlet, Little John, and the others?'

'They all say there is nothing to forgive. That I wasn't myself. But we have yet to talk properly about what happened.'

'Their forgiveness will remain, I'm sure.' Hugging Robert to his side, something he hadn't done since before he'd lost his beloved Mathilda, the earl smiled. 'How was the enchantment broken?'

'When Marion... when she kissed me.'

'There you are then.' Patting his son on the back, the earl clambered to his feet. 'You can visit me in Huntingdon any time Robert, but I will not allow you to use it as a place to hide from who you are.'

Climbing astride his horse, the earl was assailed by memories. 'Marion reminds me of your mother in so many ways. Keep hold of her; not every man is so lucky with his woman.'

Robin wanted to believe his father, but the voice of doubt kept nagging at the back of his mind. 'But what if Marion only loves me because she is conditioned to? How can I stay in the forest knowing that?'

'And that's the most evil magic of all, making you doubt the truth of your heart.' The earl turned his horse towards his home, towards Huntingdon. 'You said the spell that held you to Morgwyn broke when Marion kissed you?'

'Yes, Father.'

'Then, there's your answer, Herne's Son. There's your answer.'

EPILOGUE

'The Hooded Man, the forest, and the woman.'

The orange spark, which had almost dwindled to nothing, morphed into a soft crimson glow. As Herne watched, the flame within the brazier grew stronger, and the mists of a new prophecy began to weave together.

The Lord of the Trees gave what might have been a smile as he muttered into the smoky vapour.

'So must it be, Robin i' the Hood.'

You may also enjoy...

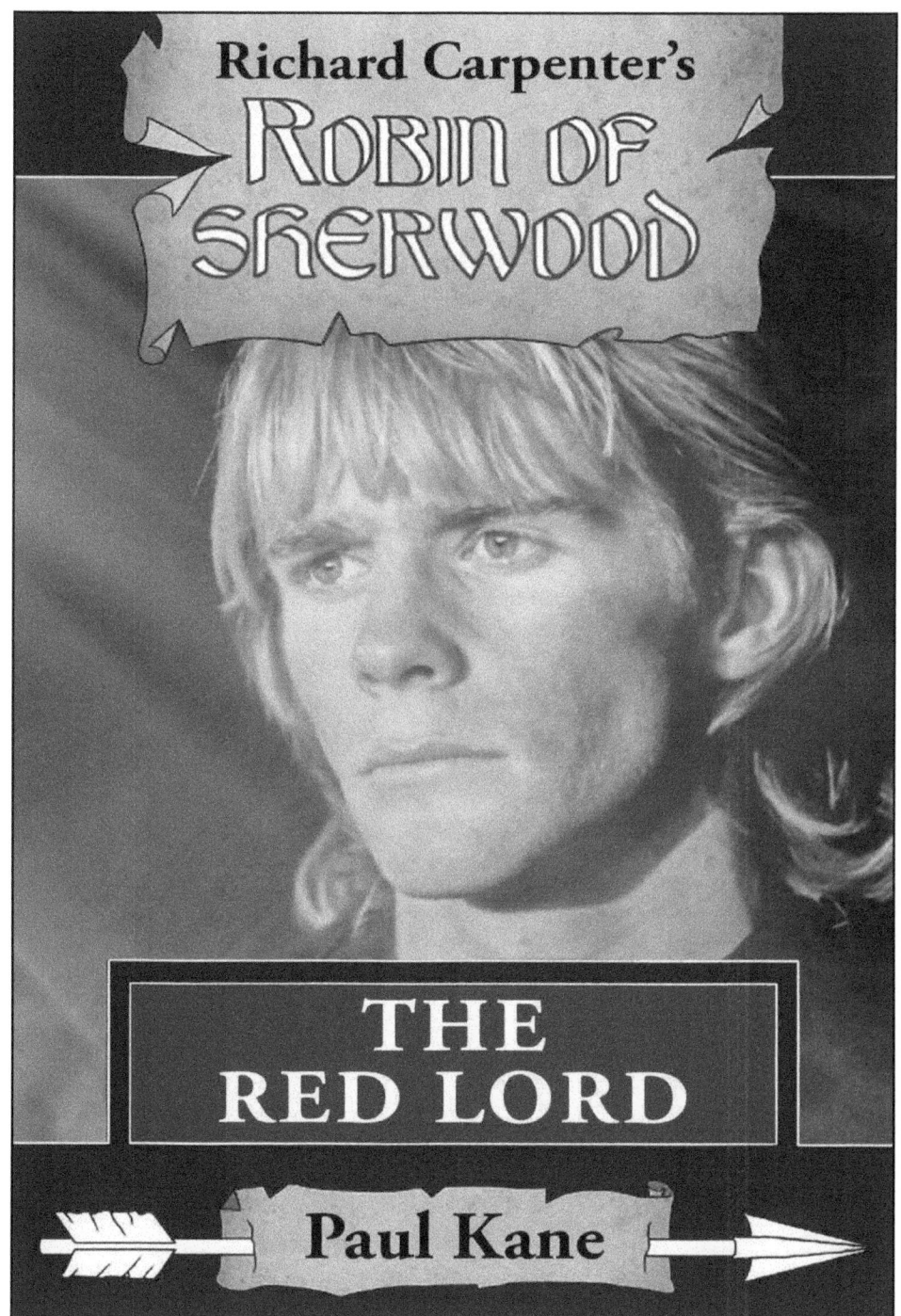

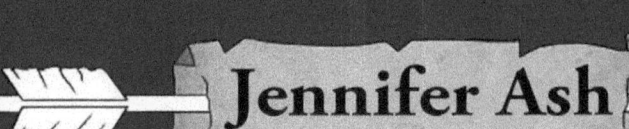

Lightning Source UK Ltd.
Milton Keynes UK
UKHW010158190322
400272UK00010B/87

9 781913 256531